MARVELRY'S CURIOSITY SHOP

John Brhel & J. Sullivan

CEMETERY GATES
MEDIA

Marvelry's Curiosity Shop
Published by Cemetery Gates Media
Binghamton, NY

Copyright © 2016 by John Brhel and J. Sullivan

ISBN: 978-1535012744

Printed in the USA by CreateSpace

For more information about this book and other Cemetery Gates Media publications, visit us at:

cemeterygatesmedia.tumblr.com
facebook.com/cemeterygatesmedia
twitter.com/cemeterygatesm

Cover illustration and design by Ben Baldwin

EPISODES

"I am sure there is Magic in everything, only we have not sense enough to get hold of it and make it do things for us."

– Frances Hodgson Burnett

THE VICTOR TALKING MACHINE

D r. Marvelry's Curiosity Shop had been a fixture of Binghampton's Antique Row since the 1990s. Early on, it had served as a magic, masquerade, and Halloween shop, full of knickknacks, party favors, and gag gifts. With the increase in competition from big box stores that sold cheap costumes and party hodgepodge, the owner, Dr. Marvelry, was forced to find a new niche. He turned what was for him a hobby—obtaining curious objects from strange, storied people and locations—into the main focus of his business.

Marvelry, having been a travelling magician for most of his adult life, had collected goods throughout North America, and gradually filled his shop with old surgical tools, bizarre electrical appliances (which usually did little more than shock or mildly electrocute its user), and began serving a younger, usually more macabre-minded and technologically savvy caliber of clientele. The older collectors still enjoyed the Victorian furniture pieces of the antique stores down the block, and scoffed at the oddities found within Marvelry's shop.

Brent and Kevin Buckley were young and in love when they came in that Saturday afternoon in late May. They were newly married and still just beginning to decorate their Rural Gothic home just over the border in Pennsylvania. They had passed through most of Antique Row, worn out from the repetitive Art Deco reproductions and post-WWII mass-produced furniture that filled the other stores.

"Well, this is different," said Brent, as he and his lover approached a surgical table repurposed as a shop counter.

"There's already so much here that I like," said Kevin. He started to hum an old show tune and flipped through an 18th-century surgical tome that sat near the antique cash register. "Hello, sirs," said Dr. Marvelry. His sudden appearance behind the counter made the couple jump back.

"Jesus," exclaimed Kevin. The pair couldn't stop laughing at Marvelry's entrance but found him to be oddly charming. The store owner had a greying dark-brown coif and a cleanly shaven face. His nose was his most prominent feature, but he was by no means ugly—more so *aged* than anything else. He was slim, above average in height, and wore a scarlet vest, vestigial (or merely in remembrance) of his old performance uniform.

Marvelry turned away and arranged his pinned butterfly showcase as the couple caught their breath. "Can I interest you in any of my new necrological jewelry? Or is it magic tricks you seek?"

"So, you must be Dr. Marvel-ree?" asked Brent.

Marvelry spun around. "Why, yes. But it's pronounced 'Marvel-rye,' no need for 'doctor,' and the accent's on the 'eye.'"

"Well, nice to meet you, Mr. Marble-rye. We're looking for some unique pieces to accent our new home in the country," said Kevin.

"That's Marvel... Forget it. So you're looking for furniture? A showpiece? I think I have just the thing," replied Marvelry as he disappeared into the rear of his store.

Brent looked at Kevin and they began laughing again. Marvelry returned a minute later carrying a heavy case. He set it on the counter, then opened it, revealing an old phonograph with a black, metallic horn.

"You're a fan of old music?" asked the magician, eyeing Kevin.

"Yes, I am. How did you..." replied Kevin, but Brent cut him off.

"That would go fantastic on the stand we got from your grandmother, Kevin!" said Brent, excited at having hit on a home design match.

"This is a Victor Victrola and it still works. It even comes with a Frank Sinatra record," said Marvelry as he set the record in place and wound the handle on the phonograph. It played a lovely song that both Brent and Kevin recognized instantly from the musical *Ashland!*

"I've never heard this version; it's stunning," said Kevin, completely enamored with the machine. He looked at Brent, who sighed, knowing it wasn't going to be cheap.

"The handle sticks from time to time, but it's really in great order, considering its age. I purchased it from a widow in Carbondale, PA, in the mid-Nineties," said Marvelry.

The trio made a deal on the phonograph and said their goodbyes. The couple left feeling like they had made a new friend.

Kevin and Brent returned home with their new phonograph and placed it in their bedroom on the mahogany stand that had been entrusted to Kevin on his grandmother's passing. They admired their new Victrola and chatted about other aspects of their bedroom that they could improve.

The Buckleys spent the rest of the weekend painting their downstairs bathroom, tilling their new garden, and moving boxes into the basement. When Monday arrived, Brent went to work at the law firm downtown, while Kevin stayed home and maintained the house.

The two-story Rural Gothic was exceptionally quiet in Brent's absence. The couple had traded the honking horns and street noise of Manhattan for the chirping crickets and solitude of rural Pennsylvania only months prior, and Kevin still wasn't quite used to it. He needed some background noise to not feel so alone.

He was dusting the bedroom dresser when he turned to the Victrola. Seeing its elegant design and simplicity made him think of mid-20th century culture—the 1940s and 50s, a time he had never experienced but held a deep fondness for. His favorite actor was James Dean; the Marilyn Monroe vehicle *The Seven Year Itch* was his favorite film. He had enjoyed the Sinatra tune Marvelry had played in his shop and thought it'd be nice to listen to again.

He turned the crank several times, adjusted the tone arm, and set the needle down on the record, smiling as a chorus of voices became audible over the cracks and pops of the vintage vinyl. Then came Frank.

"As so often goes today/at times I've forgot the way..." The song was slow, dreamlike. Kevin got so wrapped up in the moment that he just sat on the bed, forgetting the housework.

The song played on— "When I say you're the girl for me..." —and Kevin was drawn further and further in by its lilting melody and leisurely pace. He closed his eyes and completely submerged himself in the music.

At the sound of someone screaming, his eyes shot open and he jerked his head up. It sounded like a man, but Kevin couldn't make out a word he was saying. He felt as if the voice was all around him, echoing from wall to wall, surrounding him. He shot out of bed and ran to the window. There was no one outside, nobody close enough to have reached his ears, no matter how hard they screamed. The voice was suddenly joined by several others, men screaming in manic tones. Their voices were gruff, hoarse, yet quivering.

Kevin's eyes darted from the window to the open bedroom door. The sound wasn't coming from the hallway either. No, it was originating, without a doubt, from the Victrola. The record spun along, crackling. The men screamed; Sinatra crooned. Kevin was about to turn off the machine when the song concluded and the tone arm returned to its original position. All was quiet again. No more sweet melody, but no more agonized cries either.

Out of curiosity, Kevin picked up the record sleeve that lay next to the stand and flipped to the back. It looked like an ordinary Sinatra recording. Copyright 1943 Cambrian Records. Written by J. Daniel Drew. There was nothing on the sleeve about men crying out in agony. No hint that he had purchased a "funny" record either.

When Brent returned home from work that evening, Kevin recounted his experience with the Victrola over dinner.

"You've been cooped up in this place by yourself for too long," said Brent. "I told you, you need to get out sometimes. You're hearing voices now?"

"I'm not 'hearing voices,' Brent. It's on the record, as clear as day. It sounded like a group of men screaming for their lives."

"Riiiiight," said Brent. He stood up from the table and put his dirty dish in the sink. He thought Kevin was trying to pull his leg.

"I'm not screwing with you. It's the weirdest thing. I can't explain it."

"Let me hear it then."

The couple finished cleaning the kitchen then headed upstairs to the bedroom. Kevin shuddered at seeing the phonograph. He stood several feet away as Brent wound up the machine. The record began to play. The song filled the room with sweet melody, but no screaming voices called out this time. No horror could be found inside the LP's grooves.

Kevin was flabbergasted. "But I swear. I heard them this morning. Brent, they were screaming bloody murder. I'm not joking."

"You probably dozed off with it on and it found its way into your dream. Or maybe the record is just warped. Who the heck knows? The thing's ancient. But there are no voices on there other than Frank Sinatra and some backing singers." Brent left the room, annoyed by his lover's guessing game, while Kevin stared at the Victrola, wondering to whom those voices, which he was 100 percent certain he had heard, belonged.

Over the next week, Kevin tried in vain to get the Victrola to produce the strange sounds he had heard. He placed the needle at different spots on the record, turned the handle really fast, backwards, forwards, but it was all to no avail. He fiddled with the phonograph so much that one evening the handle became stuck. No matter how hard he cranked, it wouldn't budge. His investigation, it seemed, had come to an abrupt end. He went to bed with Brent a few hours later, frustrated.

As the couple slept that night, the handle on the Victrola came loose. All of the energy Kevin had put into winding it was released, and the machine fired up and music poured out of the horn. And this time, the strange voices returned, louder and more intense than before.

The couple was jolted from their sleep as the shrill screams filled the room. Brent cried out himself and grabbed hold of Kevin, who was shaking. The voices only intensified—agonized screaming and pleasant harmonies merging into a nightmarish cacophony.

Kevin pushed the comforter away, intent on turning off the phonograph, but he felt a heavy, almost crushing pressure on his chest, as if a chunk of the ceiling had collapsed onto his upper body. He remained frozen in a strained position in the bed. Gasping for air, he cried out to Brent, who was experiencing a sudden fit of coughing next to him.

The music ended and Kevin was suddenly able to move freely. He jumped out of bed, rushed over to the switch and flicked on the overhead light. Brent had ceased coughing as well with the conclusion of the song and was staring down at his hands. They were covered in phlegm. Mixed in was a black, sooty substance.

The next day, the Buckleys carried the Victrola back to Marvelry's. The horror of the previous night had convinced Brent that something was most definitely wrong with their new purchase. They wanted answers.

As they approached the counter, Marvelry appeared from behind a curtain leading to another room. "Gentlemen, back so soon? How is that phonograph treating you?"

Brent glared at the store owner and set the Victrola down hard. "Not too well, actually. What the *hell* did you sell us?"

Marvelry was taken aback by his customer's unexpected hostility. "What do you mean, sir? Is there something the matter with it? It was in perfect working order when I sold it to you."

"There's something wrong with it, alright," said Kevin. He explained the screaming voices and the strange sensations that had accompanied them. The phonograph playing by itself. The crushing sensation. The soot.

Marvelry didn't question the veracity of his claims. It was as if the store owner had heard other crazy accounts from disgruntled customers in the past. "That is one fantastic story," he said.

"That's one way to put it," said Brent.

"You said you bought it from a woman," said Kevin. "Who?"

"Like I said, I purchased it from a widow in Carbondale nearly twenty years ago. But I'm really not at liberty to divulge personal information about my customers."

Brent leaned over the counter and got in Marvelry's face. "This stupid machine nearly *killed* us last night. Tell us where you got it!"

"Alright, alright. I'll make an exception in your case, since you seem to have undergone some sort of great consternation." Marvelry opened a drawer behind the counter and pulled out a bulky, leather-bound book. He flipped to a yellowed page and scanned a list of names. "Ahh! Rose Zielewicz. Yes, Rose. I remember we had quite a lengthy chat. Nice lady. She said the phonograph belonged to her husband. He died long before that though—was it Korea? I came across her yard sale on my way to Scranton for a magicians' convention, when we still held such things. I have to warn you, she was old when we met and it's been so long, she's likely passed on herself by now."

"Rose Zielewicz. Carbondale. Got it," said Kevin, sternly.

"You're welcome to exchange the Victrola for something else. I just got in a pair of African fertility dolls. They're very unusual; great for the bedroom," said Marvelry, as the couple hurried out the door, carrying the phonograph between them.

An hour later, Brent and Kevin turned off of a country road and into the driveway at 112 Kearns Ave. in Carbondale, at the residence of one Mrs. Rose Zielewicz. Brent had quickly found her address online with the search site his law firm used to track down witnesses. It was a modest home, well-kempt, with a flower bed out front and an American flag hanging from the porch. They got out of the car and walked up the steps toward the front door, anxious regarding what they were about to ask a total stranger, especially an old widow who would probably be nervous at the sight of two unknown men on her front porch.

Brent knocked. Kevin held the bulky phonograph case. "Maybe we should've called first," said Kevin.

"*Yeah*, call some old lady on the phone and tell her we were wondering about her haunted phonograph," replied Brent.

The door opened and the two men ceased their bickering. "Can I help you?" said Rose, from behind the screen door.

Brent went to speak but couldn't find the nerve. He didn't want to sound like an idiot, or to upset this elderly widow.

"Hi, ma'am, is your name Rose Zielewicz?" asked Kevin, doing all he could to sound warm and non-threatening.

She looked at the pair with a sudden apprehension at the mention of her full name. "It is. Why?"

"We bought a Victrola that used to belong to you from an antique shop in Binghampton." Kevin held the item up to her. "Do you recognize it?"

Her eyes seemed to double in size. "Of course I do. That belonged to my husband. I couldn't stand to look at it any longer, so I sold it. And here you are, bringing it back to my doorstep."

"We apologize if it brings up any painful memories. It isn't our intention to offend you," said Brent.

"Then what is?"

Kevin and Brent were hesitant to mention the real reason for their visit. They knew it sounded crazy. Here was a woman who had no good reason to indulge them—two strangers dropping by her home unannounced with her old phonograph.

"There's something about it that isn't quite right. It's…" Kevin struggled to get the words out. "The record. There's something about it that's just off…" It crossed his mind that this visit might have been a terrible idea.

"What do you mean?" asked Rose. "What record?"

"Frank Sinatra's 'Things That I Ought to Know.'"

Rose smiled. "Ha. *That* old tune. It was one of our favorites."

"It's beautiful, ma'am," said Brent.

"What's wrong with it? It's a pretty old record. I haven't heard it in decades, in fact. Wouldn't mind hearing it again. Would you play it for me?"

Kevin and Brent looked at each other nervously. They didn't want to cause this poor woman any more pain, but she was the only one who could answer to what they were hearing. Kevin took the Victrola out of the case, set it down on the porch, and started to crank the handle.

"Ma'am, I have to warn you. The sounds on this record are unlike anything you've heard before," said Brent.

Kevin let go of the handle and the record started to play. The couple held their breath, dreading her reaction to the horrible recording. The record popped along, the needle gliding over the grooves. Sinatra started singing, the same as always. The sickening screaming, they knew, was only seconds away.

Suddenly a voice became audible within the recording. But it wasn't screaming. It was a man, and he was singing sweetly, if not faintly, as if he were serenading a lover.

"As so often goes today,
at times I've forgot the way,
but you come to me and show,
all the things that I ought to know,

When I say you're the girl for me,
you tell me to believe,
seeds we plant won't always grow,
but you will still be my rose,

People said not to bother,
with a coal miner's daughter,

whose head is off in the clouds,
dreaming of bright lights and city crowds..."

Brent and Kevin looked up at Rose. Tears were streaming down her cheeks, but she was smiling.

Kevin gave a curious look to Brent, unsure of exactly what was taking place, then looked back at the elderly woman. "That voice. Do you recognize it?"

"David," she whispered, holding her hand to her heart. "That's my husband."

Rose opened the door and invited the Buckleys in for coffee. She explained the life and death of her husband. David Zielewicz was an avid music lover. He had saved up enough money to buy a new Victor Victrola, the top-of-the-line phonograph at the time, and would take it to the mine every morning. They had a speaker system throughout the mine, and David would leave the phonograph in the foreman's office so they could listen to music during their breaks down in the shaft.

"One morning their shaft collapsed. My husband and seven other men were trapped below for forty hours before they broke through from the top," said Rose, grimly. "They had no chance. They let me and the other wives say our piece over the speaker system, in case they could hear us. I made sure they played plenty of Frank and Cab Calloway while they worked to rescue them."

Kevin and Brent looked at each other, the mysteries compounding. Did the record contain the horror of the miner's final moments and also a sweet, final message from Rose's husband? Why had they never heard his singing before?

"Mrs. Zielewicz, it was nice meeting you, but we should be heading home. You're welcome to keep the Victrola," said Kevin, knowing they would be leaving the old woman with a pleasant memory.

"Thank you. I won't mind having it in the house anymore," said Rose. She smiled and said goodbye. As she shut the door, they could hear her humming the tune, softly.

ECHO'S REFLECTION

Echo Dollinger was on her way to achieving every life goal she had set for herself. She was an associate professor of philosophy at an esteemed public university, with numerous high-profile papers to her name. The previous year, she had written a book on phenomenology and Marcel Proust that had charted on a number of bestseller lists, cementing her status as a rising star in academia. She also had a wonderful fiancé, a man named Robert Simmons.

Echo had met Robert at a local art gallery three years prior, and they had been dating ever since. He was a successful broker at Farrell Dench and the embodiment of her girlhood dreams: smart, handsome, and successful. They were engaged and looking forward to their life together, including the prospect of children.

It was a brisk February morning when Echo and Robert walked Clinton St. in Binghampton. They were on the lookout for the perfect bathroom mirror for their Neo-Victorian furnished home. They made their way down Antique Row, popping into each and every shop, but found no mirror to their liking.

They were about to give up, when they came to the last store on the block: Marvelry's Curiosity Shop. They went inside and were taken aback by the shop's odd assortment of bizarre knick-knacks and magician's tools. A skeleton key fashioned out of real bone. A cuckoo clock with a black cat that yowled the hours in place of the bird. A toy guillotine.

They had a good laugh at the items for sale, and were about to leave, when the shopkeeper strode out from the back room. "What's the matter, folks? Nothing catch your eye?"

The man made Echo and Robert uncomfortable. Where all of the other shopkeepers on Antique Row fit their expectations—upper-middle class, well-dressed, reserved disposition—this man was like a carnival barker. His eyes and smile, both wide to the point of lewdness, were enough to give them the creeps.

"I don't think you've got what we're looking for," said Echo, looking around at the strange books on the shelf: *Vivisections of Non-Vertebrates*, *A Cannibalistic History of Central New York*, *The Vortex of Rapa Nui*.

"We're in the market for a mirror. Something for the bathroom with an Edwardian sensibility," added Robert.

"Indeed," said Marvelry.

Echo was practically out the door when she caught sight of a partially covered mirror and paused. "That mirror—is it damaged?" she asked.

"Certainly not. It came from the Robertson Family. You may have heard of the museum they helped fund across town," replied Marvelry.

Echo went to the mirror and removed the silk cover to study its craftsmanship.

"So, you're Dr. Merrily?" said Robert.

"It's pronounced Marvel-'rye,' no doctor necessary," replied Marvelry. "Miss, I haven't had that mirror long. I bought it at a charity auction at the museum, just before Christmas."

"It's in great shape. What do you think, Robert?"

The man approached the mirror, then stopped. "What hideous lighting."

Echo laughed. "I never knew you to be so vain, dear."

"Don't worry, Robert. A mirror can never reveal your true nature," stated Marvelry.

"Mr. Marvel-ree," replied Echo, donning her philosopher's cap, "what could be a truer presentation of self than the apperception of one's own reflection?"

"The way you and Robert reflect each other is much more honest. Robert's beauty can never be perceived by Robert as fully as when you study him the way you do," said Marvelry.

"Sir, constructing and maintaining an image of oneself, predominantly from the feedback provided by others, is often an indication of clinical sociopathy," answered Echo, smiling. "But we'll definitely take the mirror. It's perfect."

Marvelry clapped and rubbed his hands together. "Excellent! You two have got great taste. Now, let's ring you up!" He walked back to the register. Robert followed, removing his wallet from his coat pocket.

Echo ran her fingers over the mirror's rosettes and beveled trim, imagining how it would look paired with the bathroom's rosewood cabinets. She gazed into the glass again and did a double-take when she caught an odd reflection of herself—looking to be easily twenty pounds heavier than her current weight. She examined the mirror from the side; it was neither too concave nor convex. She looked dead straight on it again, and this time the woman staring back at her appeared perfectly normal. Chalking the strange reflection up to the shop's unflattering lighting, she walked over to Robert, who was in the process of finalizing the transaction.

"Thanks again, folks. I hope this piece makes a fine addition to your home," said Marvelry, as he wrapped the mirror with newspaper and bound it in-between two pieces of heavy cardboard. "You two take care."

Echo and Robert said goodbye and carried their new possession out of the store. Robert placed the mirror on a blanket in the back of their SUV and off they drove.

When they got home, Robert carried the mirror upstairs to the bathroom connected to their master bedroom. Taking direction from Echo, he hammered an anchor into the wall over the sink, then picked up the mirror and placed it in position between a pair of cabinets.

When he removed his hand from the back of the mirror to let it rest against the wall, he jerked his head back at the image before him. A hideous purple and black bruise was running from his temple to his cheek, as if he had been severely beaten. He blinked his eyes rapidly, disbelieving, then turned back to Echo. "Honey, wha-what the hell? Did you see that?"

"What?" she said, perplexed by her husband's sudden vexation.

He looked back at the mirror, but the unsettling image had vanished. He ran his fingers over the supposedly bruised portion of his face, but it wasn't painful to the touch, nor were there any abnormal marks or lumps. "Nothing. I must be tired." Like Echo earlier, he attributed the strange reflection to a trick of the mind, a result of an odd angle.

After settling in from their shopping trip and attending to other items they had picked up that morning, Robert and Echo discussed their wedding plans. The color would be coral, there would be exactly 150 guests, and the vegetarian option at dinner would be a gluten-free pasta.

Talk of the future led, as it tended to, to the inevitable discussion of children. Echo had some reservations about staying home with their future progeny and losing momentum. She knew children would bring some form of career hiatus, an inability to write in private for hours at a time, and a break from the hallowed halls of academia. But as a woman with strong beliefs in early education, she couldn't just let them run rampant in daycare. Robert was supportive of her career, but plain biology would dictate that a woman must make certain sacrifices a man simply never has to.

The following morning, Robert left for work while Echo finished doing her makeup in front of their new mirror. Her first class wasn't until 10 a.m., so she had time to get lost in her thoughts. She didn't immediately notice her own reflection alter. She had been thinking of a few of her newly postpartum friends— their fatigue, physically and emotionally—and was pulled from her trance when she noticed that her own imagination had transformed her reflection into a sympathetic state. A weariness weighed beneath her eyes; she had even developed slight jowls! She blinked several times, then stared back at the mirror. She relaxed at the return of her normal figure. There she was again—svelte, alert, her body unmarred by motherhood.

When Robert returned from work that evening, he told her that one of his colleagues had been assaulted and robbed in the parking lot during lunch.

"Rob, you work late, and they don't have enough security around that building. Will you promise to be careful and come home a little earlier for a while?"

"You know I can't help my hours. I'll stay safe. On a positive note, I think they're going to make me a managing director soon. Isn't that great news?"

They had a nice dinner at home. Echo refrained from bringing up the topic of the mirror, her morning shock, and its psychological implications.

The next morning, Robert was up at 4 a.m. sharp, ready to start his workday. He was shaving in the bathroom mirror. The house was quiet, so quiet that he could hear Echo toss and turn in the other room. He looked down and dipped his safety razor into the water to rinse it off, quickly returning the blade to address a few errant hairs above his collar bone. When he looked up he saw a figure in a black ski mask standing behind him, as if he were ready to strike. Robert shuddered, and when he flinched, he cut his neck with his razor.

"What the heck was that?" Robert looked around the bathroom for anything that might resemble the intruder. It certainly wasn't someone at the window, as he was on the second floor. When he turned back to the mirror to check his neck wound, an eerie feeling passed over him. His face was bruised again, but this time the longer he stared into his reflection, the deeper in color and more real the blemish seemed to become. He raced into the bedroom, turned on the light, and woke Echo.

"Look at my face! The bruise is back!" he yelled.

Echo awoke in a panic at his fearful excitement. "Let me see!" she replied, somewhat groggy and unsure of what exactly was happening. "Rob, I don't see any bruise. You cut yourself shaving, and it's practically streaming down your neck. Go get a towel."

"What do you mean?! There's definitely a bruise." He hurried back into the bathroom to check his face. Sure enough, the bruise was gone, and his neck needed blotting and a bandage.

The rest of the day passed uneventfully for the couple. Echo taught class, Robert sold oil futures. That night when they went over wedding details together, they found themselves arguing over minutiae that they would normally have let pass without conflict.

"We should've hired a wedding planner. We both have too much on our minds to have to worry about table decorations and listing every single song the deejay's going to play," stated an exasperated Robert.

"This is more important than our work. This is about us and our future. We should be enjoying this time together, because soon enough we'll have to put all of our energy into a baby."

"Why? Are you *pregnant?*"

Robert's tone irritated Echo, as if he were accusing her. "No! But don't worry; it'll all fall on me anyway. You'll be a managing director at Farrell Dench and I'll be stuck at home, with my treatise on Merleau-Ponty untouched and unfinished for years."

Robert went to bed early that night. When he saw the nasty bruising return while washing up, he said nothing about it to Echo. She, too, had an encounter with their foreboding mirror that evening. While Robert slept she witnessed something unlike any previous vision. The mirror became a looking glass into a living room where a pretty toddler stood. A frumpy, overweight woman then entered the picture, carrying two screaming twin baby boys. The ragged woman was stone-faced and dead-eyed. She looked absolutely miserable, having to deal with the day-to-day grind of motherhood.

Echo tried to tell herself that she was simply projecting her anxiety over her future with Robert onto the mirror, but it looked

22

and felt so real to her. That she would become that sad shell of a woman seemed almost an inevitability, not just a possible outcome based on present and future choices she was free to make. She wanted to wake Robert and share her fears with him, but she didn't want him to think her weak-minded.

Robert's morning routine was again marred by the ghastly bruising in the mirror. He had slept poorly and thought it better to just get on with his day, rather than give the vision any credence. He left before Echo's alarm went off, wanting to give her more time before properly addressing their scuffle. He loved her as plainly and purposefully as on the day they first met. He was confident that she would be his lifetime companion, and the mother of his children, unto death.

Echo felt almost hungover from her poor night's sleep. She got ready for work with a small handheld mirror she kept in her purse, rather than again bear witness to her own psyche-made-real in her new, antique mirror. Her day wore on slowly. Not looking into the mirror was perhaps worse for her. She could only think about what it would have revealed had she looked that morning. Would it have shown her children grown and gone? Her divorce from Robert? Her own death? What horrible things would await her when she eventually looked back into that abominable metal-coated glass?

Echo didn't get any work done that day, and left the college early. By the time she got home she was sick with anxiety, and had to run upstairs to vomit into the toilet. She felt better after heaving and started a warm bath. But ultimately, she couldn't help herself and turned to look into the mirror. There she saw the living room again, this time with three school-age children at play. Echo saw herself sitting on the couch, now seriously overweight, staring at something on the TV like a zombie. In that moment she resented Robert—that he would allow her, or even pressure her, to make the life choices that would lead to the end of her intellectual life.

Echo knew she couldn't blame Robert, the only man she had ever truly loved, for the choices she would have had to make freely. She knew in her heart, that the mirror, whether a psychical projection or something more fantastic, was an honest picture of one form of her future. Dr. Marvelry was very much wrong about a mirror's inability to project an honest image. If she became Robert's wife and raised his kids, she was looking at her future, and at the end of her freedom to fully pursue her one driving passion in life—the development of her intellect.

There was no future for her without Robert; she knew and felt that as an absolute truth. The only alternative was to face the unknown, a life without him—and a life without Robert was certainly not worth pursuing. She couldn't stomach the prospect of ever living a life unexamined—just carried along into old age the same as everyone else, without routinely stopping to just be conscious of what it means to be a living, breathing being in the world.

Echo lashed out and punched the horrible mirror. Her sizeable engagement ring caused the glass to shatter into nasty shards in the sink and onto the floor. She watched the blood from several small cuts run down her hand and wrist for a few minutes. She texted Robert, "I'm sorry" before stepping into the warm bathtub, now brimming with water.

Robert, having also carried the daily anxiety of the mirror, instinctively knew from Echo's text message that she was in danger. He left work and raced home. When he found her in the bathtub, her wrists were slit and the life had drained from her face. He screamed and picked up a large shard from the edge of the bathtub, which she had used to end her life. As he wailed for his lost love, he witnessed the horrible facial bruise fade from his reflection in the mirror fragment.

Echo Dollinger was dead and buried five years when Robert Simmons finally married. He and his new wife had trouble conceiving, as they discovered Robert was completely sterile.

MAGICIAN'S COMPLEX

Dr. Marvelry had earned himself quite the reputation in the Binghampton area and beyond during his years as a performing magician. His act was the stuff of legend. In his heyday he never left a stage to anything less than a standing ovation. He had appeared at nearly every famous theater from New York to LA, from Carnegie Hall to Caesar's Palace. He was the model for many would-be illusionists, and not many magicians had met or surpassed his mastery of the craft in the two decades since his abrupt and mysterious retirement.

Peter Myers, a 35-year-old administrative assistant from the nearby village of Chenango Point, was a Marvelry devotee. He longed for the admiration and fame his idol had enjoyed—to thrill massive crowds with spectacular tricks, to leave audiences spellbound. Peter admired Marvelry so much that he had given himself a similar stage name, "The Great Maravelli," hoping that he might remind booking agents and the average Joe of the great magician.

But the similarities between Peter and Marvelry ended with the moniker; The Great Maravelli was a non-entity in the magic world. No performance halls, clubs, or casinos would book him. He performed exclusively at bar mitzvahs, birthdays, and small corporate events. And even those crowds barely paid him any attention; he was merely background noise. Truth be told, his act was sub-par—underdeveloped and sloppy. His mediocre reputation preceded him.

Peter walked into Marvelry's shop one afternoon intent on purchasing a dynamite new showpiece for his upcoming appearance at the annual Farrell Dench Team-Building Retreat. Maybe, he thought, with the right trick, he could stun a crowd for once and polish his tarnished image. He had perused the store before but had never built up the nerve to actually converse with the great Dr. Marvelry and get his advice. Marvelry was hanging an authentic Revolutionary Era Iroquois war breastplate when Peter approached him.

"Good afternoon! What brings you today?" said Marvelry. "Might I interest you in a turn-of-the-century anatomical chart?"

Peter shook his head. "No, thank you. You're Dr. Marvelry, right? The magician?"

"It's Marvel..." Marvelry stopped himself, turned, and smirked, pleased that his customer knew the proper pronunciation of his name. "Why, *yes*."

"It's a pleasure to finally meet you, sir. I'm actually a magician myself. My name's Peter Myers, but I go by The Great Maravelli."

"Ah, yes. I thought I'd recognized you. I've seen your act," said Marvelry, in a less than enthusiastic tone. He walked away from his display of Iroquois jewelry, over to a table on which lay a Charlie McCarthy ventriloquist doll. He had, in fact, seen Peter in the store before, but usually the younger man seemed too nervous and fidgety, and would leave before he could converse with him.

Peter followed the shopkeeper. "So, wha-what'd you think? I'd love to hear your opinion, sir." In reality, he was steeling himself for Marvelry to say his worst.

"My nephew was celebrating his tenth birthday down at Cross Park. It was sometime last spring. You were..." Marvelry paused, realizing he needed to choose his words carefully in order not to frustrate this eager, young magician. "I recommend you master the basics—card tricks, object replacement. I feel you might be overestimating your abilities at this point. A few well-performed standards will do you better than mucking up a bunch of advanced tricks."

Peter was crushed. "Is that so?"

"Mastering the art of magic takes time and discipline. Don't be dismayed. I spent decades on basic sleight-of-hand before I felt comfortable with the contraptions of our art."

"Thanks for your advice, Dr. Marvelry, but I don't have years to prepare. I'm performing at a corporate event this weekend and I need a good trick, something that'll really get these people to remember me. It's a pretty decent client. I think if I do well, this could really help out my career. Can you help me?"

"Come with me." Marvelry led Peter to a far corner of the shop. He felt sorry for the earnest man. Set against the wall, next to a display of ornate crucifixes, sat a large oak bureau. The shopkeeper knocked on its front doors, then turned to Peter. "What do you think? Nice, eh?"

Peter raised his eyebrows. "It's a... bureau?"

"Yes, but it's not just *any* bureau. This, my friend, is a magician's best friend. Look here." Marvelry pushed the bureau away from the wall to reveal a false back. "With this piece, you can make anything you want 'appear' with ease. Animals, objects— maybe an audience member's purse or toupee. Its mechanics are excellent, designed by a true genius of our art form."

Peter stared at the bureau. It was decorated with occult symbols and iconography and its legs sat on four cloven hooves. It looked the part, but as a functioning device for his act, it seemed a little simpler than he had imagined. But, ultimately, he decided a great magician like Marvelry knew better than him, and it could be just what he needed. "I'll take it!"

Marvelry explained to Peter in detail how to operate the bureau, informing him that it was only a revealing device, and that he must never attempt to use it to make things disappear—as it could be a very complicated, and messy, process. "It works so well, in fact, that I had to stop using it during my touring days. It made me complacent; it practically took care of the act itself. A good magician should always try and work above his skillset. Use the cabinet—have fun with it—but don't rely completely on it. Perfect the basics and hone your craft."

Peter paid for the bureau and Marvelry wished him good luck at his upcoming show. Marvelry's assistant, Drew, arrived at Peter's house later that day with the bureau in the back of his SUV and Peter helped the young man carry it inside.

Peter stood in the living room of his sad one-bedroom apartment, staring at the bureau. The fine, handcrafted item stood in sharp contrast to the disheveled appearance of his abode. He briefly practiced working the cabinet's false back and secret compartment like Marvelry had shown him in the shop. He didn't practice long before he felt a sudden rush of anxiety at the thought that the item might not be the answer to his problems, and left the room.

The Farrell Dench Team-Building Retreat was held at a country club on the outskirts of Binghampton. The grounds were a lush green and meticulously cut, and the main hall was a study in luxury. Peter arrived an hour before his set and observed the audience. This was no birthday party at Plucky's Pizza Place; this was a serious affair for adults with high expectations and little patience.

He paced back and forth in his makeshift dressing room and went over the act in his head. He'd start with a few card tricks, transition into the Chink-a-chink, and finish with the old dove pan. Basic. He just wished that he had practiced a little more.

The emcee called his name and Peter walked out to a crowd of about eighty Farrell Dench employees. Powerful men and women. His props and set pieces, including the bureau, were waiting for him on a small stage. Peter knew he probably wasn't going to incorporate the bureau into his act that evening, as he was unsure of its value or his ability to utilize it properly. But he took an unexpected comfort in performing beside it, as it had been on stage with Marvelry at many a great magic show.

"Good afternoon, ladies and gentlemen," said Peter, bowing before the audience. "I am the Great Maravelli!" Everyone sat in their chairs silently, unmoved, as if he had just said he was there to give a presentation on contemporary trends in oil price volatility.

He kicked his act off with a few of the basics. The Elevator Card and the Three Aces drew a few half-hearted claps. He followed these up with the Chinese Linking Rings, which he completely fumbled through, revealing the gap between the key ring, then dropping them.

He looked out at the crowd. People were snickering, whispering amongst themselves. Many had taken out their phones and were ignoring his act completely. The events coordinator who had hired him stood in a corner of the room, arms crossed, an irritated look on his face.

Peter froze. His dreams of being a great magician, of performing on one of the grand stages that Dr. Marvelry had frequented, were slipping away. He would never rival the brilliance and awe that his great idol had inspired. It was then, out of desperation, he remembered the bureau. It sat just ten feet away from where he was floundering, a true magician's tool.

He absentmindedly fingered the thick stack of fake money hidden away in an inner pocket of his oversized jacket. He approached the bureau, trying to think through a set-up on the spot. Distracting the crowd with a simple reveal with his right hand, he placed the bills through the false back and into the secret compartment.

"I'd like to show you a one-of-a-kind bureau," he said, opening up the front doors to reveal an empty interior. "You're probably thinking, 'An empty bureau? What's so magical about that?' And you'd be right. There's nothing magical about an empty bureau." He closed the doors and knocked twice on top of the cabinet to distract from the actual revealing mechanism he worked with his other hand. "But see, like you, I'm in the wealth creation business—and this bureau is one killer investment!"

With that he flung open the doors and out tumbled stack after stack of fresh, green Treasury-certified bills. The audience roared in laughter at the reveal (and his little dig at their money-obsessed profession.) They were amazed at the sheer volume of the seemingly real money, and many commented that there was no way all of it could have fit into the space allotted by the cabinet.

Peter, too, was taken aback by the trick. The mechanism had worked as Marvelry had described, but something else had taken place inside of that bureau, something, perhaps, truly magical. For when Peter picked up the bills from the stage, he saw they weren't fakes after all, but genuine $50 bills.

Peter was in high spirits after the show. He pocketed some of the magic money that had spewed out of the bureau and headed over to Christie's Steakhouse for an expensive dinner. But when the check arrived, he opened his wallet to reveal a wad of dummy bills. He was so happy how the night had gone, however, he didn't mind. The Farrell Dench employees who had scrambled to pick up money during his performance found that their money was fake as well. Many were disappointed that the cash was gone, but the transformation only served to make Maravelli's act that much more impressive.

The door to Marvelry's shop opened the next morning and in walked Peter, smiling from ear to ear. He approached Marvelry, who stood behind the front counter, examining a brass telescope.

"Ah, the Great Maravelli has returned!" said Marvelry. "How is that bureau treating you? Did the show go well?"

Peter smiled. "You don't know *how* well. I need to thank you, Dr. Marvelry. The bureau, well, it works wonders."

"It's a fine showpiece," said Marvelry. "A perfectly designed and mechanically brilliant magician's tool."

"It's a miracle, are you kidding me? The crowd was so astounded, word got out and I got a gig opening for the comedian Gordy Dinizio. That bureau saved my act."

Marvelry eyed Peter curiously. As far as he knew, the bureau was simply a basic, workmanlike tool. Like a "magic" hat. "I'm happy it's working out for you, young man. Just remember not to rely too heavily on one showpiece."

Peter couldn't believe Marvelry's near dismissal of what he considered to be a guaranteed career-making device. He not only planned on using it again but building his entire act around the bureau. He invited the shopkeeper to his show that Friday night and headed home to practice with his new and powerful showpiece.

The bureau, as Peter had predicted, was a surefire crowd-pleaser. His old birthday party rabbit, Ralph, multiplied like rabbits and busted out of the bureau, storming the stage. The crowd responded, cheering as the reveals became more impressive. The next time he opened the doors, dozens of doves flew over the audience and into the rafters. Next he yanked out an unbelievable amount of inflated party balloons—way too many to actually fit in a bureau of its size—and the crowd laughed and applauded.

Peter couldn't believe his good fortune. The more outrageous his reveals, the more the crowd erupted. His status as a magician was skyrocketing. He could hardly contain his excitement when he covertly placed a handful of Fourth of July sparklers in the false back. The second he opened the doors, a series of fireworks shot up and exploded over the crowd, dazzling everyone in attendance. He walked off the stage to a standing ovation. Peter grinned as he passed the comic, Gordy Dinizio, who looked appalled and upstaged. The Great Maravelli was finally living up to his name.

Marvelry stood in the back of the venue, shaking his head. Peter had relied solely on the bureau to carry his show, something he knew would only lead to disappointment. He couldn't believe the reveals that Peter was able to pull off. They were too good for a thirty-year veteran, let alone a magician of Peter's experience level. He only then came to the full realization that the bureau was more than a perfectly constructed magician's tool; the man who had given it to him, Martinus, must have been a conjurer.

Martinus, was a close friend of his former mentor, The Illustrious Dante. Martinus had given Marvelry the bureau as a way of thanking him for paying for the funeral arrangements and burial

31

upon Dante's death. Marvelry's reveals and his mental acuity at his peak were already so fantastic that he simply didn't realize the true nature of the bureau. The reveals were only limited by the user's imagination.

In the weeks following Peter's performance, word spread that a genius new magician had arrived on the scene, and that his act was unparalleled. The Great Maravelli was the hottest thing since Dr. Marvelry; many news outlets even noted the similarity between the two men. Peter's star was shining so bright, in fact, that the Binghampton socialites behind the annual Thomas A. Zopp Cystic Fibrosis Awareness Dinner hired *him* to perform that year instead of Marvelry, who would normally come out of retirement annually to perform at the benefit.

Anyone who was anyone in Binghamton was at the benefit. It was a black tie affair held in the ballroom of the Robertson Museum. Marvelry was invited, as he was a prominent local celebrity and philanthropist in his own right.

There was an assortment of antiques from the museum's collection up for bidding. Marvelry often bid on a few items for his shop, even if they weren't so peculiar. An ornate mirror caught his eye while he was talking with the long-winded Mayor Petcosky. He excused himself and went over to check the item's opening bid. When he approached the mirror he thought he caught sight of complete chaos in the room behind him, and he had to check over his shoulder to make sure it was an illusion. He became further intrigued when he saw a few more flashes of a frenzied roomful of Binghampton's high society reflected, as he wrote down his bid.

"Dr. Marvelry! I'm so happy you could make it," exclaimed Peter, grabbing the older man by the arm and patting him on the back. "I think even *you* will be impressed by what I have planned for tonight."

"Peter, you must be careful with the bureau. There is more to it than even I knew. I believe it was made by a conjurer, a friend of my late mentor—"

"Sir, I believe I've mastered its mechanical and theoretical workings, there's no need to worry," replied Peter.

"You don't understand, Peter. It's dangerous to operate a hexed bureau," said Marvelry.

Peter eyed his mentor, suspiciously. "Oh, I get it. You're upset that they chose *me* to perform this year. You were a great magician, Marvelry..."

"Stop! This isn't a trifle. The bureau should be destroyed before it's misused and harms someone."

Peter laughed off what he mistook for petty jealousy on Marvelry's part and left the ballroom to prepare for his performance. He stood behind the curtain on the ballroom's stage, awaiting his cue. He listened closely as a father and his two children discussed the recent loss of their mother, Theresa Pachia, to the terrible disease. His heart broke hearing the young children's sobs and remembrances of their wonderful mother.

The family finished speaking and there was a brief inter-mission. Finally, Mayor Petcosky introduced The Great Maravelli. Peter strode onstage as the curtain rose, his head held high, more confident than he had ever been in all of his years performing.

The Great Maravelli proceeded to amaze the citizens of Binghampton, making one spectacular reveal after another—a live toucan, a four-layer cake (which was served to the front row by his new assistant, Becky), 500 red roses. He had the crowd in the palm of his hand. He felt like he had mastered the bureau; now was his time to pull out all the stops and prove to himself and the public *all* that he was capable of.

His energy at an all-time high, he walked off the stage and over to the Pachia family. He picked up a framed photo of the deceased Mrs. Pachia from the center of the table and started talking with the crowd about the disease and the suffering this poor mother must have endured. He was overcome by emotion—the weight of the disease and the newfound immensity of what he and the bureau were capable of. The audience was rapt. He walked back onstage and around the bureau, continuing a passionate and rambling speech about disease, death, and rebirth.

When he walked back in front of the bureau, the photo in the frame was missing. "This horrible disease has taken its toll, but we can do something about it. *I* can do something about it!"

Peter pulled open the bureau doors. The room fell silent. Slowly, a hand reached out from the dark interior of the bureau, then a full arm, a head. It was a woman, wrapped in a winding sheet. To those who knew her, the woman was instantly recognizable as Theresa Pachia, deceased six months. The crowd gasped. Several of the city's most prominent screamed in shock.

"Mom?! Is that you?!" The Pachia family ran up toward the stage, a look of bewildered joy on their faces. Peter smiled. Not only was he pulling off incredible tricks, he was reuniting a family. In a matter of weeks, he had gone from failed magician to legendary conjurer.

The Pachia family hurried up to their mother, who was now walking across the stage, the white sheet dragging behind her. Tears were streaming down the children's faces; their mother had returned. But as they approached her, close enough to see the vacant look in her black eyes, they knew that something was wrong. She neither spoke nor responded to any of their calls.

Mr. Pachia reached out to touch his wife's face, but the ghoul that merely resembled Theresa Pachia lunged toward him and bit his arm. The widower screamed and the crowd echoed his cries. In seconds, the entire room had erupted into chaos, well-dressed men and women running toward the exits, falling over one another.

Before the simulacrum could make another move, two security guards ran onto stage and dragged her away from her maimed husband. The ghoul clawed at the air like some yet-to-be exorcised abomination as they strained to hold her arms down.

Peter stood aside, shocked, watching the horrendous scene unfold. His perfect moment, his rising star, had been snuffed out in a matter of minutes. He only looked up when he saw Dr. Marvelry hop onto the stage and assist the security staff in stuffing the ghoul back into the bureau. She gnashed her teeth and made inhuman noises as her limbs and torso bent to accommodate the bureau's opening.

After closing the bureau, Marvelry turned each of the door handles inward, which resulted in a sharp clicking noise. When he opened the bureau seconds later, the ghoul was gone.

"Thank you," said a shaken-up Peter. "I don't know what happened."

"You let your ego get the best of you," said Marvelry, talking to the man like a teacher to an insubordinate student. "And you took the easy way out, relying too heavily on this device. Didn't I warn you?"

Peter nodded. "Yes." He was too ashamed to utter another word. The room had finally emptied and wound down into a still silence.

Marvelry laid his hand on Peter's shoulder. "You'll learn. First you must make your apologies—many, many apologies. I'll deal with the bureau. And while you make your amends with the people you've harmed tonight, study and practice the art. Someday you'll get your chance to perform again."

Peter thanked him one last time for stepping in and quelling the chaos, and the two said their goodbyes.

Marvelry picked up the mirror he had won at the auction earlier that night and headed for the door. The old magician paused at the exit, looking back over his shoulder. "And, Peter...don't try and raise the dead ever again!"

THE PAINTER'S PREMONITION

It was mid-afternoon, after a furious, alcohol-fueled painting session, when Justin Loza stumbled out of his studio apartment and made his way toward Harry's Oasis. His license had been revoked three weeks earlier due to his latest DUI charge, and he was forced to walk several blocks to his favorite bar. He had $100 to his name until the following Friday, and he was determined to spend some of it entertaining himself that evening.

He walked a few streets before stopping on the sidewalk, befuddled. Although he had made the half-mile trek to Harry's dozens of times, he couldn't remember which turn to take, and he was having another one of his headaches, the sort that made him forgetful from time to time. He found himself standing outside of Marvelry's Curiosity Shop. Seeing the owner inside closing up, he went in to ask for directions.

"This is an odd place, guy," said Justin, taking in the balsamy scent of the store.

"Yes, correct! I specialize in oddities, strange objects, macabre books, and antique irregularities," stated Dr. Marvelry. "Are you the sort with an eye for jewelry?" He swung a mammal vertebrae necklace in front of Justin.

"No, no. I'm lost. *Bones?*"

"Yes! Squirrel and raccoon," said Marvelry, matter-of-factly.

Justin looked at Marvelry strangely. "I'm looking for Harry's Oasis. Isn't it on this block?"

"No. Wrong direction. You need to head west."

"Oh, thanks. That easel, is it old?" asked Justin, pointing at an easel that held a painting with an abstract take on Goya's *Witches' Sabbath*.

"Yes, an antique. Are you a painter?"

"Some of the time."

"Then perhaps you'll appreciate these handmade squirrel hair brushes," said Marvelry, as he reached behind the easel and retrieved a cup of old paint brushes. "Free of charge—whether or not you have any further interest in the easel."

Justin eyed the brushes curiously. "You can never have too many of these."

"The easel itself belonged to *Timothy Kahn*."

"Timothy Kahn? I love his work in the Catskills. He was a true successor to the Hudson River School."

Marvelry smiled, but only briefly. "Yes, he was quite a talent. If only he'd picked up the brush more often than the bottle. I purchased the easel from his widow's estate sale years ago, back when I was a regular on stage at the Orpheum in Tannersville." He pointed to a small spot on one of the legs, where the letters "TK" were carved. "See? He even carved his initials."

"Cool. How much is it?"

Justin worked out a weekly payment plan with Marvelry. After paying the first installment, it left Justin enough cash to get drunk a few more times until his next check arrived.

Marvelry told him how to get to Harry's, and Justin left carrying the easel under his arm and the brushes in his jacket pocket. The regulars teased him for bringing an easel into the bar, but Justin got adequately liquored up and had a good time.

Justin rolled out of bed the following morning, head pounding, and trudged up to Dimmock Hill, his favorite spot for painting landscapes. The rolling hills and variety of mature trees of the area were intoxicating; he had sold several paintings depicting its natural beauty.

He rested the easel on a level patch of damp grass, took out several tubes of paint and his new squirrel hair brushes, and set to work painting a maple which stood out from the tree line. Despite his aching head and slight nausea, he painted swiftly. His newly acquired brushes glided effortlessly over the canvas, marking it with rich and vivid hues—phthalo green, alizarin crimson, Prussian blue.

Nearly three hours had passed before he stopped to observe the fruits of his labor. When he looked down at the canvas, however, he saw an entirely different scene than the one he had intended. The focal point was a large oak tree, wide, with low-hanging branches. The tree was situated on an open field of tall, brown grass, a clear blue sky overhead.

Justin blinked and shook his head in some vague attempt to recalibrate his brain, but it was to no avail. The picture looked nothing like the landscape he thought he had been painting, depicting an iron-grey sky and dark, oppressive clouds. Frustrated and uneasy, he gathered up his supplies and headed home.

He was three beers in that night when the phone rang. "Hello?"

"Hi, Justin." It was his mother, and her tone immediately told him that she was displeased.

"Hi, Mom. What's up?"

Mrs. Loza sighed. "Aren't you wondering why I'm calling?"

Justin searched his short-term memory, which was like navigating an unfamiliar house in the dark. He couldn't come up with any good reason for her to call other than to catch up. "No."

"You said you'd stop by last night. I waited for hours. I tried to call, but you didn't pick up."

"Mom, I'm sorry. I was..." He was about to tell her he was out at Harry's, but bit his tongue. "...I forgot."

"You really need to see a doctor, Justin; your memory is getting worse and worse. I'm worried about you."

"I will. My insurance is a little iffy at the moment, but when I get the coverage I'll set up an appointment."

The line went silent for a few seconds. "I'll pay for it, Justin. Just make the appointment. Okay?"

He said goodnight to his mother and he looked across the room at the curious landscape on his canvas, fearing he may be losing touch with reality.

The following day, he returned to Dimmock Hill and set his easel up in front of the same tree line, intent on painting the actual scene in front of him. Each stroke was deliberate. He studied the lines of the maple tree, focusing on the rough bark, the leaves scattered about the ground, the twisting, crooked nature of the branches.

But, like the day before, he looked at the painting after an hour or so to find the landscape was again the same lone oak tree. This time, he noticed a patch of daisies sprouting from the ground a few feet from the tree's roots. He couldn't believe his eyes; he was certain he had been painting a maple tree with bright-red leaves. The maddening image put an end to his session. He took the painting home and went to Harry's for the evening, hoping a few drinks would subdue the unsettling feeling brewing in his stomach.

Aaron Thurber, the owner of the popular Thurber Art Gallery downtown, stopped by Justin's apartment the next day. Mr. Thurber had recently sold three of Justin's paintings to an international collector, and he was there to present the artist with a check, as well as to find out what new pieces, if any, he was working on.

"Mr. Taito is pleased with your pieces and is ready to buy more," said Mr. Thurber. "What are you working on?"

Justin, who had ingested most of a bottle of rum before Mr. Thurber's arrival, stood up from his couch, clumsily, and led the dealer to his unfinished and unexplainable landscape painting.

"It's marvelous," said Mr. Thurber. "So realistic, like I'm really there. Where *is* this place?"

Justin hesitated. As far as he knew, the tree only existed in his mind. "Uh, over on Dimmock Hill."

"Is that right? Hmm, it looks a bit flat for Dimmock Hill. Anyway, when do you think you'll be finished with it?"

Justin told Mr. Thurber that he could complete the painting in a week. After saying goodbye to the art dealer, he returned to the painting to study it. It was, as Mr. Thurber had described, almost photorealistic, and a bit beyond what he knew to be his technical limits; it looked as real as any actual oak tree. He wondered how he had managed to paint the same fantastical scene twice. He had worked under the influence hundreds of times, and never had he managed to fool himself into painting anything other than what lay before him. Even during his year-long Cubist period, one could still see the intended subjects beyond the polygons.

The painting angered him. A distant, mostly forgotten head injury and alcoholism had plagued him for years, and this enigma only served as a reminder of his deficiencies. Using vegetable oil, a palette knife, a hair dryer, and some fine sandpaper, he removed the contemptible painting from the canvas, leaving it white and ready for another, more unassuming piece.

Justin was used to having surreal dreams, fueled by copious amounts of alcohol, but the dream he had that night was unlike any he had experienced before. He was standing in a field of dry, brown grass. The sky was a bright orange. From seemingly out of nowhere, a white horse appeared, its nostrils flared, hooves beating hard against the ground. It was running directly toward him. He turned to run himself and saw that he was facing the solitary oak tree from his painting. He sprinted toward the tree, the mustang quickly gaining on him. He was seconds from being trampled, when the horse suddenly stopped, whinnied, and collapsed on the ground.

Justin woke up, panting, his head pounding. He threw himself out of bed and dashed to the easel. Without thinking, he covered the blank canvas with paint. It was an hour later, when he put down his brush and observed the finished piece. The image was as he expected, the same lone oak tree that he had painted before. But this painting offered a new perspective on the scene. A red barn,

41

concealed by the tree in earlier depictions, now appeared off in the distance. Confused and exhausted, Justin fell back asleep, this new image burned into his brain.

The following morning, Justin awoke to knocking on his door. He looked at his wall clock; it was 11 a.m. and he wasn't expecting anyone. He walked up to the door and looked through the peephole. Seeing it was his good friend, Tim, he opened the door.

"Hey, buddy," said Tim, smiling.

"Hey." Justin looked confused.

"Did you forget I was coming over? I tried texting you a bunch of times so you wouldn't forget, but I guess you did. Who would have thought?" Tim grinned.

"Sorry. Come on in."

Tim was a fellow artist and the two talked about a new Warhol exhibit at the Robertson Museum over lunch. As was usual, however, the conversation quickly turned to gossip.

"Did you hear about Mark Samson?" asked Tim.

"No." Justin hadn't heard that name in years. Mark had been a classmate of theirs at Binghampton High.

"No? Well, he *died* last week."

"Really? How?"

"OD'd."

Justin shook his head.

"How many of our classmates have died from drugs now? A dozen?" asked Tim.

"Something like that," said Justin.

"Let's see. Eric Charles. Don Kaat. Greg Carpenter... You were lucky, though, Justin. All those DUIs. Driving drunk to school, even. Crazy. You could have been one of them, buried in Valleyview Cemetery."

"Yeah, maybe." Despite still being alive, Justin felt like another Binghampton High loser.

"Then there's Nick Zulinksy, of course. Can't forget ol' Z-dog."

"Yeah." Nick had been one of Justin and Tim's best friends growing up. He had disappeared during junior year and was never heard from again. The conversation had gone to a dark place, and the two sat in silence before Tim asked Justin what he was working on. Justin showed him the strange landscape with the oak tree and the red barn.

"Nice work. God, your use of negative space has really improved." Tim studied the painting further. "Hey, I *know* this place."

"You do?" Justin thought for sure Tim was pulling his leg. "No way you know that place."

"Why do you say so? I've seen that barn before. This is out on Day Hollow Road, right? I drive past it on my way to work sometimes, when the highway's jammed."

Justin and Tim had been friends for nearly two decades. Whereas Justin would never have told a stranger about his weird experience with the painting, he felt that, somehow, Tim would understand. He told Tim how he had never actually been to the location. How he had been painting one scene yet ended up painting another one multiple times. How he had thought it all existed in his fractured mind.

Tim was hesitant to accept Justin's explanation—it sounded insane—but being a good friend, he agreed to drive out to the location and prove to Justin that it was, in fact, a real place.

"Buddy, you must've driven past the barn and oak a few times on the way to the bowling alley," said Tim. "Everyone forgets stuff, even those of us with good memory."

Tim's white Ford Taurus wound through the desolate, dirt roads of rural Binghampton. Justin felt a strange anxiety as they neared this supposed location. He wondered what awaited him. He was overwhelmed, that he could walk along a field and gaze upon a tree that he was sure he had never seen, yet knew so well that he could recreate the shape and texture of the branches in exquisite detail.

He turned to Tim. Something about driving out on that road with his friend felt oddly familiar. He had been on many country drives in his wild teenage days, but never with Tim and never on that road, as far as he could remember. But as the car beat down Day Hollow, it was if he had seen these exact hills and trees before.

"We're almost there," said Tim.

Justin's head started to throb. The anticipation, coupled with a strange feeling of déjà vu, threw him into a mild panic attack. His heart beat rapidly. He seemed unable to adequately inhale. He looked back at Tim but froze. Justin saw himself sitting in the driver seat instead, albeit a younger version of himself. And the interior of the car, somehow, had transformed into that of his old '92 Mustang. He watched as this teenage version of himself took a swig from a flask and stomped on the gas. Up ahead, the lone oak tree came into view. It was true; the tree actually existed. And they were heading straight toward it.

"Stop the car!" screamed Justin. Suddenly, he was back in the present and Tim was sitting in the driver seat. Tim hit the brakes and the car came to a screeching stop. Justin looked out the front window. To his surprise, they were still on the road.

"Jesus, Justin! Are you alright?" asked Tim.

Justin sat in his seat, silent. Up ahead he spotted an old oak tree in an empty field. A barn could be seen in the distance. He felt a deep, aching feeling in his stomach. "The *tree*."

"Let's go take a look," said Tim.

The two friends got out of the car and walked toward the oak tree. They were miles from any home or business. The pasture had long been abandoned, and the silence was palpable. The closer they got to the tree, the more Justin's head pounded, until it felt as if someone were bashing his temple with a dull mallet.

They were about five yards from the tree when they saw something long and white sticking out from the ground, just a few feet from a patch of daisies.

"Looks like some bones, dude," said Tim.

Justin didn't know why, but he felt that these were not the remains of any farm animal. "It's probably some horse or cow bones," he said, lying.

He looked over at Tim. The sudden change on his friend's face—eyes wide, mouth twisted, lip quivering—told Justin that Tim also knew that these probably weren't animal bones. Justin thought briefly about the easel and the squirrel hair brushes he had used to create his painting, wondering what role they played in this horrific unraveling episode.

Tim knelt down. "Justin, are these *jeans*?" He gently tugged at a patch of denim sticking up from the wet earth. More long bone and deteriorating denim were revealed. A red Levi's tag was visible on the fabric, although the woven text was now illegible. "Justin?"

Justin didn't say a word. Yes, they were jeans. They had belonged to their good friend, Nick Zulinsky, Z-dog. And Nick had disappeared; this much was true. But what Tim didn't know, and what Justin had only suddenly, and painfully, come to recall, was that Nick had died on the very road they had come in on.

Nick and Justin were drinking and cruising around in Justin's Mustang when Justin lost control of the vehicle and landed in a drainage ditch. Nick, who wasn't wearing his seatbelt, was ejected out of the open passenger window. Justin hit his head on the steering wheel; the concussive force shook him and he lost all memory of the night—the night which brought about head trauma, memory loss, and headaches for years to come. In a drunken panic, shaken from smashing his head, not considering his or Nick's future, Justin drove his friend's body out into the field. He found a shovel from the distant barn and used it to dig a shallow grave for his friend, under the lone oak tree.

Standing there, staring at the bones of his old friend jutting out from the ground, it had all become crystal clear.

"Justin? Justin!?" Tim shook from head to toe as his friend gazed vacantly at him.

A GIFT UNGIVEN

"Happy Father's Day!"

Tom Kopp held up the Iroquois bone breastplate he had just received from his son. "It's great, Chad. Really cool. Where did you get it?"

"Jenny and I were on Clinton Street looking for a couple of chairs and wandered into this weird shop. Marble-ree's, or Marvel-eye's or something. Just a real odd antique store, run by that old magician that used to be on Saturday morning TV when I was a kid," replied Chad.

"Oh, yeah, *Marvel-ree's Odd Emporium.* I've stopped in a time or two," said Tom, a professional anthropologist. He ran his fingers over the piece. "This is authentic. It might even be Revolutionary Era."

"Yeah, it wasn't cheap, Pop," replied Chad, grinning. "The owner said he bought it off a carnie in Horseheads not too long ago."

"Huh, strange," said Tom. "It's certainly old. I'd say it's a Mohawk war plate based on the design. And it looks like it's seen a battle or two." Tom pointed out some gashes in the bone ribbings.

"I figured you could use it for some of your interpretive classes at the battlefields."

"That'd be perfect. I can't wait to show Dr. Rogers. She knows Mohawk design much better than I do. Which reminds me—check out the necklace she gave me for my birthday." Tom pulled an intricately beaded necklace from under his shirt. "It's authentic Kanaweola, very rare."

"Nice. So, are you and Dr. Rogers an item now?" asked Chad, smirking.

Tom's face turned red. "It's not like that, buddy. We're work colleagues, and friends."

Chad and his father had lunch and played a round of golf that afternoon before Chad returned to his own family. Tom had been divorced from Chad's mother for years and lived alone with his dog, Leakey. He rarely dated, and relied on work colleagues and his only child for companionship. He poured all of his attention and time into his teaching job at Binghampton College, where he was an associate professor of anthropology with a specialization in Haudenosaunee and Tuscarora native culture.

That week he showed off his new Iroquois relic to his colleagues and students. Dr. Eureka Rogers verified that it was, indeed, an authentic Revolutionary Era piece. Tom was excited to do an interpretive day for his Indigenous War Cultures class at the nearby Newtown Battlefield. It was the site of General John Sullivan's victory against the British and Iroquois forces and a real turning point for the Continental Army.

He gathered his students in the school's big passenger van and drove them out to the state park battlefield. When they arrived, he donned his authentic Iroquois props, including the new breastplate.

"On this hill, the Haudenosaunee were determined to make their final stand against the colonists, who had been pushing them westward since the Dutch began claiming land west of the Hudson," said Tom, sternly. "General Sullivan marched along the Quee-hanna and Chemung rivers with thousands of soldiers, burning the crops and villages of the Six Nations. The Iroquois had to choose between losing their land to the colonists or dying at the hands of the Continental Army, and they chose to fight."

Tom had his students rapt; they watched him proudly stroll about with musket in hand, hatchet at his side, in full Iroquois war regalia. "The British and Haudenosaunee readied their battlements on this hill, hoping to ambush Sullivan's army on the road and push them into the river. But Sullivan's scouts spotted the ambush and he devised a plan, executing a wide flanking maneuver and overwhelming the Loyalist and Indian force. The hill ran red with British and Haudenosaunee blood, and the Six Nations' back was broken...here on this very hill."

The professor paused and his students clapped. He answered a few questions and then gave them a break to wander about and visit different areas of the park, as clouds were rolling in and it looked like it might soon rain.

Tom was hiking by himself in the woods on the hillside when he thought he saw someone shadowing him. He knew every ranger that worked the park and was sure none would have any issue with him doing a little off-the-map exploration. He walked and listened to the eerie silence of the forest before turning abruptly. Tom caught sight of a bare-chested figure behind bush and branches about fifty yards off, just before the figure drifted away.

"Hey, what's up? Are you lost or something?" Tom could've sworn it was a man—and that he had most certainly been watching and following him.

The first cracks of thunder rang out over the river valley. The professor felt the air change and knew a hard rain was imminent. He started jogging back toward the main path to gather up his students, when he spotted the figure in his peripheral vision keeping pace with him. Tom kept jogging, but he felt an oppressive presence around him and a tightness in his chest, which he wrote off to the change in pressure from the oncoming storm.

When he reemerged onto the paved park path, he looked back, with a nervous agitation, but saw that the bare-chested man hadn't followed him out of the woods. The man kept enough distance that Tom couldn't make out much about him, but it was obvious that the stranger wasn't hiding the fact that he was stalking him.

"Okay, everyone, back in the van, time to go. Are we all here?" said Tom to his class, who had begun milling about the parking area as soon as they heard thunder overhead.

The rain poured down and lightning flashed every few seconds as Tom guided the van back toward Binghampton. He couldn't help but wonder about the mysterious man in the woods and his intent.

That evening Tom had a lucid dream about the Newtown Battlefield and the scenes he had been describing to his students. He was in one of the battlements with musket at ready, side by side with a British infantryman, as Continental soldiers from New York and New Jersey streamed in. Smoke enveloped him, inhibiting his senses. He had a hard time keeping his weapon trained as orders were yelled around him in English and the Seneca and Cayuga dialects.

The battlements were being overrun. Tom could see bayonets flashing; the Continental soldiers were readying to strike. He braced himself for the final assault, his whole body quivering. He dropped to the dirt on his back as a bayonet was thrust toward his chest.

But before the bayonet could find its home, Tom awoke abruptly in his bed, the sheets soaked in sweat. He realized he wasn't one of the brave Haudenosaunee who had given their lives in a last-ditch effort to impede the inevitable destruction of the Sullivan-Clinton Campaign. He got out of bed, intending to go to the kitchen to get a drink of water. When he left the bedroom he paused mid-step. At the end of the hallway, outside what used to be his son's bedroom, stood a bare-chested Indian. Although it was dark, he immediately thought of the man from the battlefield. Now merely yards away, he could see the intruder's shaved head and painted face and associated the presentation with that of a regional tribe that he could not quite place.

Tom shuddered, unable to move or speak. The figure approached. A sliver of light spilling from his bedroom revealed a weapon in the stranger's hand. The professor backed away, a wave of panic rushing over him. As the intruder raised his axe, Tom's German Shepherd, Leakey, came rushing up the stairs, barking. The native suddenly vanished, confounding Tom.

The following morning, Tom sat, uneasy, in his office in the anthropology department. He wondered why had he been visited twice, seemingly by the same spirit.

Eureka Rogers entered, smiling, but stopped when she saw Tom's gloomy demeanor. "What's wrong, Tom? Rough night?"

Her light presence pulled him from his ponderous thoughts. "Eureka, I think I'm losing my mind."

"What's up?"

Tom was infatuated with her, but wasn't sure how much he wanted to tell her about his menacing Indian spirit. "I'm probably getting a little too into character—I dreamt I was one of the slaughtered Haudenosaunee in the Battle of Newtown."

She laughed. "Jesus, Tom. No one is as dedicated to their work as you, and you're a real asset to the college. But maybe you should take some time off, go on a fishing vacation or something."

"I do like to fish."

She smiled at him, and he momentarily forgot about his ghostly worries. He gathered enough courage to ask her over for dinner that night and she accepted his invitation without hesitation.

Eureka arrived at Tom's that evening and the two sat down for dinner. Tom couldn't remember the last time he had enjoyed a home-cooked meal with a woman. They talked about work, family, and future plans. Eureka had also gone through a messy divorce and had never quite built up the courage to put herself into situations where she might get serious with another man.

She and Tom had been colleagues and friends long enough that she hadn't immediately recognize her growing feelings for him. As she readied to see him that evening, she considered the possibility that she could easily, and happily, begin a serious romance with him.

"Corn mash soup. Mmm. This is delicious, Tom," said Eureka. "Is this your own recipe?"

"No, I learned it from a Tuscarora tribesman. It's one of my favorites."

Eureka smiled and took another spoonful.

When she looked up from her bowl, however, she practically tumbled from her chair in shock. Standing behind Tom, bare-chested and holding an axe by his side, was a war chief. It was such a random, incomprehensible image, she could hardly believe her eyes. But when she watched the Indian raise the weapon above Tom's head, she screamed and dropped her spoon in the bowl, splashing broth all over the table.

"Tom! Behind you!"

Tom, startled, spun around in his seat, but saw that no one was there. "What? What is it?"

Eureka described the man in detail. His chest was bare and brawny; a scraggly scar, which looked like it could have come from a bear encounter, ran across it. There was a thick band of black paint across the man's eyes, while his forehead was covered in white. Large rings dangled from his ears, and he bore a necklace of long, jagged teeth. Tom told her that he had seen the same man before.

They talked briefly of the indigenous legends regarding shamanistic conjuring, curses, and ghosts. But ultimately, both being academics of sound mind and reason, the thought that this man was some sort of actual native spirit seemed too ludicrous a theory to pursue. The experience had soured their date, however, and Eureka left a half hour later.

Still, Tom couldn't help but wonder if his ghostly stalker might be connected in some way to his new breastplate.

After teaching his Introduction to Archaeology course the following morning, Tom drove across town to Dr. Marvelry's shop to get some answers. When he walked inside, the owner was dusting a leather gun holster.

"Excuse me. My son purchased this for me a few weeks ago, and I have a few questions about it." He removed the breastplate from his bag and showed it to the shopkeeper.

"Ah, yes. Your son. I recall he came in with a female companion. I tried to sell him a set of dentures owned by P.T. Barnum, but he wouldn't *bite*." The man chuckled, but Tom didn't react. "What do you want to know?"

"Where did it come from? He said you bought it from a roustabout?"

"Yes, the seller worked the coconut shy at the Waverly Fair, I believe."

"Did he mention anything strange about it when he sold it to you? Did he talk about seeing anything or anyone after putting it on? A spirit?" Tom couldn't believe he was asking another grown man such questions.

Marvelry chortled. "No, sir, he did not. Although, that would make for a curious object, wouldn't it?"

"Well, do you know if it's genuine or not?"

"I can't say, sir. Unfortunately, I am no expert in Native American artifacts." Marvelry paused as something caught his eye. "However, I do recognize that necklace you're wearing, and I'm certain it's authentic. I purchased it from a local Indian, and it was an heirloom of theirs. They were very sad to part with it."

"Really?" said Tom, surprised. He thought of Eureka and their spoiled first date. He looked around the cluttered shop and saw a few more native trinkets, even some Cherokee and Lakota items.

"Yes, you sir, are very lucky to have such giving people in your life—because I can assure you, neither of your items were cheap. But again, of the breast piece I've no further information. Maybe you should talk to someone at the college, perhaps?"

"Yeah." Tom's hopes were dashed.

Marvelry admired the breastplate. "It looks authentic enough. I've always wondered about the previous inhabitants of this land. They say there was a great battle not too far from here where the natives made one last stand against our army. Maybe I should take a class..."

That's when it hit Tom. "Yes, Newtown Battlefield! I started seeing the spirit when I wore it at the *battlefield*." Outside of the combat zone, the breastplate had been merely a primitive form of armor. But on the battlefield it had triggered something, awoken something ancient. "Thank you, Dr. Marble-ree." He left the store in a hurry, as the shopkeeper shrugged and returned to his tasks.

Tom immediately called up Eureka and convinced her that he had an actionable plan regarding his apparition: He would go to the battlefield and return the breastplate to the place where the haunting began. Eureka, fearful that the vengeful Indian spirit might harm her friend, insisted that she accompany him.

They arrived at the battlefield that night as another heavy rain beat down. The deep rumble of thunder and the mad flashes of lightning reminded Tom of cannons and musket fire. So much blood had been spilled on that ground, and he did not want to join the ranks of the deceased Loyalist and Iroquois forces. His heartbeat quickened as he got out of the car, breastplate in hand.

Tom and Eureka walked toward the top of the hill, fighting a heavy wind. The rain was hard and cold. A flash of lightning lit up the park and they could have sworn they saw the outline of a man in the distance.

They were nearing the top of the hill when a beam of light shone over them and a voice shouted, "Hey, what are you doing out here?!"

They turned to see a park ranger standing some distance away, holding a flashlight. "The park closes at dusk, folks!"

"Let me handle this," said Eureka to Tom. "I'll tell him you lost your watch or something."

"Thanks," said Tom and he winked at her.

Eureka walked down the hill to talk to the ranger while Tom continued his ascent. When he was out of sight of the ranger, he removed the breastplate from under his jacket and held it toward the sky. "I'm giving this back! D'you hear?! I'm giving it back! I respect you, your sacrifice, and your people!"

Thunder cracked as Tom set the breastplate down on the ground. Relieved, he turned to meet back up with Eureka. A wave of relief washed over him as rain drops streamed down his cheeks. It was over, finally over.

Hearing a shrill scream, Eureka and the ranger hustled up the hill.

"Tom?! Tom?!" she called out as she struggled to run up the slippery grass.

When she reached the crest of the hill she shrieked. Tom was lying on the ground with a hatchet in his back. He lay lifeless, his clothing sodden from the rain.

But Tom wasn't alone. Eureka watched as the native removed the axe from his back, then bent down. He unsheathed a small knife and brought it down toward Tom's neck. Eureka cringed, unable to call out or will her legs to move toward the scene. Tom was clearly dead—she could see blood streaming from the horrific axe wound even from twenty yards away—but she was terrified by what the spirit might do next.

The Indian pulled one end of the necklace away from Tom's neck and cut it off. The breastplate was still in Tom's hand when the native disappeared; the spirit didn't want it after all.

The ranger appeared at the top of the hill, out of breath. "Ma'am, what's wrong?" he asked, panting. Then he saw the body.

"It killed him," said Eureka as the rain fell on Tom's cold body.

The ranger pulled out his gun. "Huh? Ma'am, what happened? Who did this?!"

Only then, looking down at Tom's lifeless body on the very hill which he had focused so much of his time and attention, did she put it all together. The spirit was that of a Kanaweola Indian. Seeing the breastplate on Tom, it had mistaken the harmless anthropology professor for a Mohawk warrior. The necklace belonged to his people, and he was simply retrieving stolen property from a man he believed to be a sworn enemy. A necklace *she* had given him.

No one would ever believe her.

A MADE MATCH

Marsha Frampton stared at a pair of wood carvings with large, disc-shaped heads set on an open bookshelf inside Marvelry's Curiosity Shop and called to her husband, Allen. "Honey, check these out."

"What are they?" he replied, busy admiring a collection of vintage *Weird Tales* magazines.

"I don't know. They look strange, though," said Marsha." Each carving was about eight inches tall. One man, one woman. They were sculpted in a somewhat awkward fashion, with comically exaggerated extremities.

Marsha had her eyes fixed on the male doll (and his disproportionate phallus) when the proprietor's face appeared between the statuettes, grinning at her. She jumped back and squealed, partly in embarrassment.

Dr. Marvelry stood up, laid his hands on top of the bookcase, and leaned forward. He was so close, Marsha got a good whiff of his citrus-scented cologne. "They're African fertility dolls, ma'am. All the way from Ghana."

Marsha eased up. "Fertility dolls?" She looked intrigued.

"Akuaba, handcrafted by the Ashanti people. Well received the world over," said Marvelry, raising his eyebrows in a provocative manner.

Marsha looked over at her husband. Seeing he was pre-occupied, she turned and whispered to the shopkeeper. "Would these work to improve a man's, umm, stamina?" she asked, blushing slightly.

"Perhaps," said Marvelry, a wry smile crossing his face. "Likely more effective than the promise pills and herbal remedies one comes across on late-night TV."

"Well, they're really neat looking. And I wouldn't mind any *added effects*. How much are they?"

Marvelry revealed the price, which caught Allen's attention and prompted him to saunter over.

"That much for two little dolls?" asked Allen, bending down to inspect the carvings. Marsha rolled her eyes at her husband, who would haggle over the price of a candy bar.

"These *dolls* hold immense power, sir. The people of Western Africa have turned to them for centuries as a reliable reproductive aid."

"Oh, I'm sure," said Allen. He looked back at his wife, and he knew *that* look. If he didn't budge, she'd be on him for days. "Okay, how much for just one of 'em?"

"Sir, the woman I bought these from was adamant that they be sold as a pair—as their power comes from their proximity, their union." Marvelry's countenance became suddenly serious, his eyebrows furrowed.

"That's great, but I'm not dropping one-hundred bones on some imported trinkets."

"*Allen,*" said Marsha, looking at her husband sideways.

"We'll take one. The lady," said Allen as he handed his credit card to Marvelry.

At first Marvelry hesitated and considered turning down the man's offer. But ultimately, he wanted to please his customer, so he cheerfully wrapped up the statuette in brown paper and placed it in a plastic bag. "Enjoy. But I make no promises that this doll will have any positive impact on your fecundity, or love life, for that matter. Good day, ma'am. Sir."

The Framptons left and Marvelry spent the next hour doing paperwork and setting up a meeting to sell a 19th-century straight jacket to an up-and-coming magician he knew from a nearby hamlet.

He was just getting off the phone when another couple, Lindsay and Jeff Buckingham, entered the store. Marvelry greeted the thirtysomething pair, who said they were there to purchase a magic set for their son.

"Magic! Why, you couldn't have come to a better place!" said Marvelry.

"So we've heard," said Lindsay, who had been referred to Marvelry by a member of the Binghampton Rotary. "So, what do you suggest for a budding young magician?"

Marvelry led the couple to a shelf lined with wands, hats, scarves, handcuffs, and other staple props. He showed them some of the classics—the torn and restored fifty-dollar bill drew a smile from Lindsay—and put together a solid starter set for their son.

Pleased with their selections, Jeff and Lindsay followed the shopkeeper to the register. They were about to complete the transaction when Jeff noticed the remaining fertility doll on the shelf. "What's this thing?" he asked, pointing at the small wooden man. "Is this another magic prop?"

"That, sir, is an African fertility doll," said Marvelry as he placed a set of false playing cards into their bag. "Magic of a *different* sort, you might say."

"Is that right?" said Jeff, a mischievous smile crossing his face. He turned to Lindsay. "Honey, that could come in handy, don't you think?" Lindsay shrugged and scowled at her husband.

Jeff turned back to the shopkeeper and said in a low voice, "Let's just say it's been a while."

Without a response—Marvelry was a gentleman, after all—the shopkeeper went over to the shelf and removed the doll. He wrapped it up and placed it in the bag. "As a thank-you for purchasing this magic set, I'd like to give this to you as a gift."

Jeff smiled. "Wow, thank you, sir. That's really nice of you."

"We don't need that, Mr. Marvelry, really," said Lindsay, who thought the doll a hideous little thing, and was quite content with her sole child. It really had been a while.

"Honey, c'mon," whispered Jeff to his wife. "It's a nice gesture."

"Whatever," said Lindsay, in a huff, and took the bag from Marvelry. Jeff followed her to the door, but not before turning back to the shopkeeper and slyly grinning.

Marvelry waved goodbye. He was pleased. While the starter set had been expensive, he had mainly given the doll away out of discomfort. He thought the unpaired statuette to be bad luck and wanted it out of his shop as soon as possible.

The first couple that visited Marvelry that day, the Framptons, had by now returned to their childless home, and placed their new doll on a shelf opposite their bed.

"I love it," said Marsha, standing back a few feet from the shelf, admiring her new purchase. The exotic, dark-brown doll stood in sharp contrast to the bedroom's simple, peach-colored theme.

Allen shook his head. "That thing's weird. And why do we have to have it in the bedroom? Is it going to undo your hysterectomy? Couldn't you put it down in the living room with your other tchotchkes?"

"It's not just supposed to make a woman pregnant, Allen. It's supposed to be an aphrodisiac of some sort for women *and* men. Where else would we put it, on the porch?"

Allen groaned. "You're kidding, right? That doll's gonna give me a stiffy? *Sure.*" He left the room.

They were lying next to each other in bed that evening—Marsha doing her crosswords and Allen watching baseball on TV—when Marsha felt her husband's hand run up her thigh.

"Allen!" said Marsha, giggling. He hadn't made a move on her in months and she thought he was still upset about the doll.

He began to kiss her neck. "Yes, honey?" He continued, adding another hand to the mix.

"Hey, are you sure you're up to it? After what happened *last time?*"

Without saying another word, he took hold of his wife and made sweet, fervent love to her. Marsha was overwhelmed by Allen's sudden endurance; it was like he was twenty again. She closed her eyes and experienced a pleasure she had previously given up the possibility of. The room suddenly felt warmer, stifling almost, as if someone had cranked up the thermostat. Allen's thrusts were so zealously ordered, heartfelt, that she nearly passed out following her peak moment.

Across town, Jeff Buckingham set his and Lindsay's fertility doll on their bedroom dresser, next to a bottle of his favorite cologne. "Look, honey. Maybe this will help with our little problem."

Lindsay, who was hanging up a modest vintage dress she had picked up from one of Antique Row's more reputable stores, turned and looked at the doll with disgust. "*Blech.* It belongs in the trash. And we don't have a *problem.* You just have a dirty mind."

"Honey, it's been almost a *year.*"

"What did I tell you? I don't want to talk about it. I just need time."

Jeff sighed. "Yeah, you keep saying that."

Without a response, Lindsay left the room.

Later that evening, Jeff brushed his teeth, got into bed, and cracked open one of his legal thrillers. His nose was buried deep in the book when the bedroom door opened and Lindsay walked in wearing flimsy lace lingerie with scarlet straps, highlighting a shapely body she normally kept hidden.

"Honey?" asked Jeff. He was caught completely off guard.

"Hey, baby." Lindsay smiled seductively, a simper he hadn't seen in ages. She walked slowly toward the bed. Jeff sniffed the air, thinking she might be drunk, but she hadn't had a lick. She got in bed and the two explored each other in uniquely unrestrained ways. As with the Framptons', the Buckinghams' room became almost unbearably warm, their ardent interactions engulfing the room with their body heat.

Fifteen minutes later, they were lying on their backs, sweaty and out of breath. Jeff exhaled deeply and smiled. He was about to fall asleep, when Lindsay suddenly straddled him. She wanted more, and she got it. Then twice more in the middle of the night. She was insatiable.

Before passing out from exhaustion around 3 a.m., Jeff looked at the fertility doll standing on his dresser and grinned. He didn't believe in magic, but it certainly hadn't been a mood killer, that was for sure.

The next several months were blissful for both the Framptons and the Buckinghams. Their marriages, which had grown frustrating and lifeless, were suddenly reinvigorated.

Marsha was physically fulfilled for the first time in years. Allen pounced on her every night, and she reciprocated his passion. Eventually, his drive became so intense, however, that she was having trouble keeping up with him, and left him many a night wanting more. She thought about the fertility doll and wondered whether if, in some way, it really was working. Allen's erectile dysfunction and sluggishness in the bedroom had soured their love life for some time, and he had suddenly, almost miraculously, been cured and acquired the stamina of a man twenty years his junior.

She picked the tiny, wooden woman off the shelf and held it in her hands. Her fingers ran along the grooves of its eyes and over its nubby chest. *Surely, nothing so small, some piece of wood, could have any real influence on her life, could it?* Dr. Marvelry had told them that it derived its power from being paired with the other doll. *Even if magic or any sort of mumbo-jumbo like that did exist, the doll shouldn't work anyway, right?* Out of nowhere, she felt a sudden fire in her loins, an unexpected desire to touch herself. She looked down at the doll and a fear swept over her. Her hand was shaking as she placed the carving back on the shelf and left the room.

Unfortunately, it wasn't long before Allen began acting strangely, heading out for late night walks, hiding phone conversations in other rooms. She started to suspect that he might be sleeping with other women to sate his extraordinary libido. Marsha had heard of sex addiction and Allen had been exhibiting the telltale signs. As quickly as their marriage had improved, it again languished due to the specter of Allen's infidelity.

Meanwhile, the Buckinghams were starting to have problems of their own. Lindsay's desire had grown so strong; much more than Jeff could handle. She uncharacteristically began returning the flirtations, and then eventually, the advances of a coworker. She didn't feel her normal, reserved self anymore, and it was exciting. Soon Lindsay was staying late at work a couple nights out of the week, and heading out to the market at all hours of the night.

Jeff suspected Lindsay was up to something. Not a month before he had called her a "cold, frigid bitch" to his buddy. Now she was practically a hedonist.

He was waiting at the kitchen table at 11:30 one night when Lindsay strolled in, a wide smile across her face.

"Have fun...shopping?" Jeff asked, his voice cutting the silence of their home.

Lindsay gasped. "Jeff! What are you doing up?"

"Oh, you know, I was just thinking how nice it would be to fuck my wife. But I suppose Bryan in marketing is already fulfilling that role for me." Before she could lie her way out of it, he took out his phone and showed her an email she had sent her coworker, complete with a photo of her bare breasts.

Lindsay started sobbing. "Jeff, honey. You don't understand. Something's come over me. It's like I'm possessed or something. Like somebody turned on a switch. I just want to get off day and night now. Nothing satisfies me anymore." She revealed to her husband that Bryan was only one of the three men she had been with that week alone, and that she had already made plans to meet with a new guy the coming weekend.

Jeff went to bed alone that night; Lindsay took the sofa. When he looked across the room at the fertility doll, his face twisted into a scowl. Like Marsha, he didn't exactly believe it to be some hexed artifact, but it did remind him of his wife's betrayal. He stomped over to the dresser and picked up the carving. In the dark, the doll's grotesque features and oversized head took on a nightmarish quality, as if it had been fashioned by some malevolent artisan. He threw it at the wall, but it bounced off with a loud thud and fell to the floor, completely intact.

Within weeks of visiting Dr. Marvelry's shop, both the Buckinghams and Frampton marriages were unrecognizable.

Lindsay, her infidelity already out in the open, went on what could only be described as a sex spree. She made the rounds of every major dating site, meeting up with dozens of men, practically emasculating them with her ferocity and sexual prowess. But no matter how many men claimed to be up to the task, she couldn't find her equal in the bedroom.

She was perusing Cupid's Arrow, a site for casual encounters, when she came across a profile for a newer member: Allen Frampton. What caught her eye were the number of negative reviews and messages he had already accumulated in his short time on the site, and that he proudly displayed on his front page: "Sex was great. He wasn't;" "He's a player, ladies;" and so on. A couple of chat sessions later, Lindsay was in bed with the man, pushing him to his limit, and he hers. Their encounters were animalistic in their intensity and disregard for societal norms. Their "sessions" became so frequent, so cataclysmic, that they both called into work sick, morning after morning, to keep their streak alive.

Weeks passed and, mistaking their lust for something of substance, Allen and Lindsay revealed their relationship to their already defeated and disgusted spouses, professing their devotion to each other. Separation papers were issued not long after.

As their family lives crumbled around them, Allen and Lindsay decided it best to just move in together. Each brought a fertility doll to their new apartment, as their ex-spouses couldn't stand the sight of the idols. The dolls were a pair once again, side by side, in the couple's new bedroom.

What had seemed like the most passionate, wild relationship imaginable just days and weeks before, soon deteriorated into a singular monotony. Allen, who had attained the stamina of a raging bull, suddenly had performance issues, suffering what he jokingly referred to as "stage fright." Lindsay, on the other hand, grew depressed and reverted back to her old self, disinterested in intercourse, thinking it a chore.

It wasn't a month before the couple called it quits, both of them realizing that their relationship was founded on nothing. By then, it was too late to go groveling back to their spouses. The separations had been made legal, and Marsha and Jeff didn't want to hear a word from them.

On the day they moved out of their still-new apartment, Allen and Lindsay tossed their respective fertility carvings—symbols of love and family, not lust—into the trash and went their separate ways.

THE LETTERBOX

The three-story Victorian mansion in Downtown Binghampton owned by Charles and Candace Reilly had been a home away from home for Josh Hart during his childhood. He spent numerous long weekends and summer vacations there, enjoying his Grandma Candace's delicious apple pie, fishing with Grandpa Charles in the Chenango Creek. He held sacred the memories formed at his grandparents' home; they provided comfort as he grew and experienced the doldrums of adulthood.

Josh grew up. Grandpa Charles passed on, then Grandma Candace not five years later, and the estate was sold. Josh wanted to purchase it, to make his boyhood escape his own, but he was just a freshman in college at the time, with no money to his name.

The house passed between owners as Josh finished school and began his career. He kept an eye on the property, watching the old Victorian fall into disrepair as it lay empty, and eventually into foreclosure. By the time it hit the city auction block, he was in his early forties and had established himself and his finances. With no real responsibilities, he was able to secure the house for a modest price, as he had no serious competition.

As soon as the deed was his, Josh set about recreating the home as it had existed when he was a boy. He wanted to relive those days, to recapture the immeasurable joy he felt during his childhood. Unfortunately, most of the antique furniture and fixtures had been sold to shops and at auction during the many changes of hand and the eventual foreclosure. The cherished memories of his childhood guiding him, he made his way around town, following leads from different antiques dealers, collecting missing pieces of the home.

He had successfully restored a few of the lost items and furnishings, when he strolled into Marvelry's Curiosity Shop one evening after work. His eyes wandered past a collection of exotic taxidermy mounts and focused on a vintage letterbox hanging on the wall. It was a rich red, and a brassy patina had formed on the metal surface. There was a strange, ornate molding on the front. A series of apocalyptic winged demons stood out beneath a depiction of the Mormon angel Moroni. It was just as he remembered—he had found his grandma and grandpa's old mailbox.

"Excuse me, sir. Can you tell me where you got this letterbox?" Josh asked the shopkeeper, who had been instructing an assistant on a delivery when he walked in.

Dr. Marvelry smiled and came over. "That letterbox was owned by the Reilly's. A well-to-do local family."

"Charles Reilly was my grandpa," said Josh, proudly.

"Is that so? I went to school with his boys. He came in here every so often. Used to bring his daughter along with him sometimes, too, a real sweetheart. She was quite a bit younger than her brothers." Marvelry scratched his chin in an inquisitive manner. "What was her name? Margaret...Mary..."

"Molly," said Josh. "That was my mom."

"That's it. *Molly*. How is she doing these days? It's been probably forty years."

"She passed unexpectedly a few years ago, sir."

"I'm sorry to hear that."

The room fell quiet until Josh explained his quest to return his grandparents' home to its former state, how the letterbox was one of many pieces left to the puzzle.

Marvelry pulled the letterbox down from the wall and let Josh inspect it. Holding it in his hands made Josh feel even more nostalgic.

"I haven't seen Tim and Tom since they went on their mission. How are your uncles these days?"

"They're doing well. They live in Salt Lake City with their families."

"Have you gone on a mission yourself?"

"No, I heard enough horror stories from my mom and dad growing up. Besides, I dropped out of the Mormon faith when I was a teenager." Josh thought back to the summer he left the religion behind. It was right around the time his mom and dad got divorced.

"Well, we can't all take on the faiths of our fathers. We are a much too inquisitive culture to fall into the same patterns of behavior."

"You got that right."

"So, the letterbox?"

"I'll take it, Mr. Marble-ree," said Josh, without hesitation.

"Of course. And do just that. *Take it*, no charge."

Josh looked at him, unsure if he heard the man right. "No charge?"

"I didn't pay much for it. Take it to your family home and put it back where it belongs. You've got quite the task ahead of you, Sisyphus."

"Wow, thanks, Mr. Marble-ree." Josh was beaming, astonished at the stranger's generosity. The letterbox couldn't have been that cheap, judging by the price tags on many of the other items in the shop. He thanked Marvelry again and left the store with much more than he ever anticipated finding.

Josh hung the letterbox outside his grandparents' former home, next to the front door, as it had been when he was a boy. It looked absolutely perfect.

When he returned home from work the following evening, Josh lifted the letterbox lid and looked inside. Along with an ad from Barker Auto, he found a poorly handled envelope. It was addressed to his grandparents from his mother and postmarked July 8, 1974—Papua New Guinea.

He wondered how an envelope so old had found its way into the box, unopened. He was certain he had inspected it inside and out the day before. Josh had to assume he somehow overlooked it. But why would his grandparents not have opened a letter from their daughter to begin with?

He removed the stray letter and took it inside to inspect the contents. Carefully, so as to not damage a part of what he now considered family history, he slid a letter opener along the top of the envelope and made an even cut across.

He took out the letter and started reading:

July 7, 1974

Dear Mom and Dad,

I can't believe my mission is nearly over! I have made such close friends. The new temple is coming along and will be finished by summer's end. We have a strong relationship with the Islanders, and they have a keen interest in the gospels and the prophets.

Remember David Hart? You met him in Provo? His family lives in Scranton and his father's a bishop? We've grown so close. Mommy, don't let Daddy read this part: I think he's THE ONE! I never would have thought I'd meet my future husband on a mission. He's amazing. We've so much in common and have so many plans for when we get back home.

The weather's been so humid, as you'd expect of the tropics. The bugs have been pretty unbearable at night, though. I think my bunkmate, Gretchen, is literally covered head to toe in bites. She has been having constant nightmares too, so I haven't gotten the best sleep the past few weeks. They've been giving her tons of pharmaceuticals because they're afraid she might be coming down with malaria, or maybe hepatitis.

Since I've written last, we've taken two trips. One back to Port Moresby to get check-ups at the clinic and pick up supplies, and one across the water to Kokopo. Kokopo was fantastic! The Islanders did their dances and performed some incredible rituals for us. One woman even let me wear some of their traditional clothing and chanted some sort of prayer. Unfortunately, not every Islander has heard the Word of the Prophet and taken it into their heart. But they're good people, regardless!

Give my love to Nana, Papa, Timmy and Tommy, Uncle John and Aunt Sybil, and throw Scooter some extra table scraps for me!

Love Always,
Molly

Josh's mom had told him many times about her travels abroad, but he enjoyed seeing a first-hand account of her experiences. To read about his mother at just 21 years of age, falling in love with his father and excited for the life ahead of her, was a real treat for him. He placed the letter carefully back into the envelope and went about his evening.

A few weeks passed, without much thought of the mysterious letter or its contents, when Josh was startled to open the letterbox and find another note from the past. He couldn't believe another had appeared. Curious, he opened the weathered envelope, removing the yellowed notebook paper, and read:

July 31, 1974

Dear Mom and Dad,

Gretchen's health has gotten much worse. They sent her to a hospital in Australia. A few nights ago she began shaking, and I think she had a seizure. She was sweating horribly and screaming when they took her to Port Moresby. I don't feel sick exactly, but I've been having the same wretched nightmares as her. I imagine a demon with terrible yellow eyes comes to the bunkhouse each night and asks me if I want to meet the prophets, and he tries to tell me about my future.

I know this is a very real deceit that I have to deal with, this last month before I return home to you all. I don't know if I have the courage. The demon threatens you all and David if I don't listen to his horrid stories. And it feels so real that I have to remind myself that it's only my own weakness. I need to focus on the mission and less on life after the mission. I've told David we should spend the last month apart, and get the most out of our individual spiritual efforts before we are sealed for eternity.

The Indonesian army has been poking about, asking the mission leaders what we're up to and hassling us. The temple will be built soon, and the local Islanders will keep the Word of the Prophet close to their hearts. They are few, but they are proud!

Love Always,
Molly

P.S. I'm sorry my letter was so short. I love you all more than words, and will see you soon enough!

Josh finished reading, perplexed. He wondered who was sending him the old letters, and why. He thought about calling his dad, who lived hours away with his new wife and family. But the two had a falling out and hadn't spoken in years, and he didn't want to contact him out of the blue to ask about a couple of letters from his dead ex-wife.

Over the next week, Josh thought continually about his mother's nightmares. Her description of the strange, yellow-eyed demon was unsettling, even if it was just a dream, and he couldn't shake the image.

He checked the letterbox every day, anticipating another mystery envelope, but found nothing out of the ordinary. A month passed and no other letters arrived. He had given up thought of receiving a third letter, when he returned home from a day out and discovered another deteriorated envelope in the box. He looked around, as if the source of the letters might be standing idly by, watching him, waiting for his reaction. Seeing no one, he went inside and opened the letter:

August 19, 1974

Dear Mommy,

I address you and only you in this letter because you've known me to always be truthful in all matters. Daddy will assume the worst, and I'd rather deal with him face to face. I'm begging you for your forgiveness, Mommy. I thought I was strong, and spiritually mature enough to keep the Deceiver away.

You have to believe David and I have kept our word and our mission. He and I have spoken very little these past few weeks, and haven't hugged or kissed or even held hands. The Blasphemous One came each night and promised to prepare me for all of the hardships I would encounter. I refused him, but he wore on me. He showed me visions of my brothers at college, and you and Daddy safely at home. But of the future—I've seen a tragedy for the Islanders, for our family even. I don't know what to do or say regarding all of it.

I let him lie with me in return for the special knowledge. I needed to know everyone I love would have long, happy lives. You all do, Mommy! Tragedies will come, but they're so impersonal they're not worth putting down on paper. I know I've sinned against you, Father-Elohim and the Prophets, against David. Oh, David. I don't know that he'll understand, or that anyone will think me anything other than a lunatic.

I make my worldly confession in hopes of worldly forgiveness. I will strive every day to live in your image of piety, and become a sister worthy of membership at temple.

Love Always,
Molly

Josh read the letter again and came to the realization that his mother was attempting to conceal an undeniable truth—she was pregnant with him. Why would she make up such a far-fetched story when it was obvious that she was sleeping with his soon-to-be father? After all, he was born nearly nine months after the letter was written. He had never known his mother to be a liar. He did wonder, however, about the motivations of the person sending him these letters. What was their intent?

Josh found himself driving aimlessly that evening, the contents of the letters consuming his thoughts. Before he knew it, he was in his father's driveway in the town of Palmyra. He walked up to the house and knocked on the door, his mother's letters in hand. He was unsure why he had made the three-hour trip, and couldn't recall much of the intervening hours.

David Hart opened the door, a look of surprise on his face, which he quickly masked with an inauthentic smile. "Josh… Hey, what are you doing here? Road trip? It's great to see you, Son."

Josh didn't waste any time. "Dad, I need to talk you about Mom. Do you know anything about these letters?" He held the old, weathered envelopes up to his father.

Seeing that the letters were addressed from his ex-wife, David invited Josh inside. They both sat in silence while David read. Josh watched his father's expression change, growing increasingly dour as he made his way through each of the three letters. By the time David finished, it was clear he was disturbed by what he had read.

"Dad, why did she write these? What is this all about?"

"Josh, she wasn't lying when she said we didn't sleep together during our mission," said David. "I knew she was pregnant, but married her anyway—I loved her… And I love you." The older man paused in the gaping silence before releasing his heavy burden. "You are my son—just not biologically."

Josh was aghast. To find out he wasn't his father's son at the age of forty was too much for him to digest. "What? Are you *serious*?" He stood up and paced the room.

David nodded. "It was all pretty tough on her. There was backlash; many of her friends, and even some of her family, shunned her. It was a difficult marriage, Josh. Her demons followed her home, so to speak."

"Then who's my *real* father?"

David was unable to provide any more clarity. After a few more awkward minutes, he bade his son goodbye and Josh drove home in more turmoil, and with more questions, than when he set out.

Exhausted from the long drive home, Josh went straight to bed.

He dreamed horrible things that night—of his mother in the jungles of Papua New Guinea, copulating with an oily-skinned, winged creature. Her eyes rolled inward as she writhed with the hulking diabolus. The image was so sick, so reprehensible, that he woke in a cold sweat, shaking.

Josh sat up. The room was eerily silent. His stomach dropped when he heard something move in a corner and saw two yellow eyes emerge from the darkness.

"Welcome home, *Son*," said a deep voice, its true form still concealed by shadow.

Josh awoke from the nightmare in the early morning light, grasping at his bed sheets. He burned his mother's letters, giving up on his mission of reconstructing the old Victorian and his family's past.

SEAMS OF CONSEQUENCE

The needle of the vintage sewing machine bobbed rapidly, puncturing coarse fabric, as Emma Cowden pushed her foot down on the cast-iron pedal. Todd's job at the electric company, climbing utility poles and repairing blown-out transformers, put more stress on his jeans than the Lee company had ever intended them to endure, and a large hole had begun to form along the inseam.

As she pushed the well-worn fabric through the machine, she dwelled upon her middling existence; she was 36, living in a shoebox of an apartment, unwed, and insignificant. Todd was a good man—hardworking, kind—but his meager salary afforded her none of the luxuries of which she sought. To be respected. To be seen. To be comfortable.

The needle was pecking away at the fabric when Emma suddenly heard a loud pop. She looked down to see that not only the needle, but the whole mechanism—from pedal to drive belt—had broken. She burst into tears, desperately pumping the pedal, tugging at the bunched-up denim, but it had finally happened—her grandmother's machine had sewn its last stitch. The couple couldn't afford to keep buying new clothes, and Todd would be forced to wear his shabby jeans, walking around like some working-class grunt. Not only that, but with the machine inoperative, she couldn't do the one thing she was really good at.

Hearing Emma's cries in the cellar, Todd hurried downstairs from the kitchen to find his partner hunched over, her head resting on the sewing machine cabinet.

He drew up next to her and gently laid his hand on her shoulder. "Honey, what's wrong?"

Emma didn't look up. "My machine's broken," she said, her mouth quivering.

"Let me give it a look." Todd fooled around with the pedal and tried his hand at fixing the machine, but his expertise lay solely in power cables, transformers, and the like, and he was unable to do a thing.

"Don't bother. When the iron's bent like that it's useless," said Emma.

"You're probably right..." He paused, thinking. "Listen, you can buy a new one if you want, okay?"

"But, babe. On *our* budget?" She had recently been laid off from a seasonal department store job.

"I'm not saying go out and buy a brand new one or some expensive antique. But I'm sure there's someplace you can find a cheap-enough replacement."

Emma wrapped her arms around Todd and smiled. As she was wont to do in situations that revealed his good nature, she brought up the topic of marriage.

"Honey, you know we can't afford that now," said Todd. "A sewing machine is one thing. Listen, someday when I get a promotion, I'll—"

She pouted at him like a petulant child. "You've been saying that for three years. The only ladders you've been climbing are on telephone poles."

Todd sighed. "Can we talk about this some other time? I'm bushed." He walked away to eat hamburger casserole for the third day in a row, leaving Emma to lament her lackluster existence.

That weekend, Emma went downtown to look for a new machine. An hour into her hunt, she walked into Marvelry's Curiosity Shop. She was barely through the front door when she saw it: a 19th-century Singer treadle sewing machine. It had a black, cast-iron base with a foot pedal and an ornate, oak cabinet with six gilded drawers. Floral decals covered the actual machine, which was black and well-cared for, save for a few stray scratches.

"Excuse me, sir. I have a question about that Singer," said Emma to the shopkeeper.

"Yes?" replied Dr. Marvelry.

"Does it still function?"

"I think so, ma'am. But it's well over a hundred years old. It likely hasn't sewn a stitch since Nixon was in office. Do you actually plan on using it? Most folks just buy them for decoration these days."

Everything about the machine looked in order from her brief inspection. "I've been sewing since I was a child. My mom handed her machine down to me when I turned eighteen—but it broke a few days ago. I need another one."

"Well, this would certainly be a worthy replacement. The previous owner was from a line of successful seamstresses."

Emma lit up at the knowledge of the past owner. "Oh, really?"

"Yes. The Alcott family once owned a fashionable women's clothing store. It was actually located across the street where the bodega is now. The Alcott's designed and sold dresses for debutante balls, proms, various formal events."

That was all Emma needed to hear. She *had* to have the machine. Maybe some of that good fortune would rub off on her, she thought. "How much is it?"

Marvelry revealed the price, which caused Emma's enthusiasm to drop.

"That's a bit more than I can afford."

"Hmm."

"It's just...my boyfriend and I are having a bit of money trouble. I was just laid off, and it's hard for blue-collar people to find good work in Binghampton, you know?"

Marvelry paused and eyed the Singer before turning back to Emma, a pitying look on his face. "Ma'am, that machine has sat in my store for years, and you're the first person to pay it any attention. How about we assume that it isn't working and cut the price by 70%? Would that work for you?"

Emma couldn't believe the offer Marvelry was making; she knew the value of the machine. "Are you serious?"

Marvelry nodded, smiling.

"It's a deal!"

Emma found her new sewing machine to be not only in good working order, but even better than her original. It worked so well, and she felt so confident in knowing that the previous owner had been a successful seamstress herself, that she decided to sew a dress—a wedding dress. Despite Todd's apprehension, she longed for that transformative moment, and the title and position of "wife."

Day after day, while Todd was at work, she put in the time. The dress was the picture of elegance, with Chantilly lace, and a sweep train.

The day she placed the final stitch, Todd came home, got down on one knee, and proposed. It seemed that his beloved grandfather, who had passed just the week before, had left him a modest inheritance—enough to cover a wedding and a nice engagement ring. She stared at her new prize, then rushed to the bedroom to show her now-fiancé the dress she had been working on in secret. It all felt so serendipitous.

The couple was married six months later and Emma enjoyed the attention she received. For Todd, the only thing that sullied their wedding day was the absence of his grandpa, who had been his childhood idol. They enjoyed a blissful honeymoon; however, it wasn't long before Emma began to grow frustrated yet again. Marriage was only the first step. Her status had improved, sure, but everyone else her age was having kids. She needed a child of her own.

Unfortunately, the same issue that had once prevented her and Todd from getting married returned to cast an ugly shadow over her family plans. Todd was concerned that they didn't have enough money to support a child. Not only that; but he had been tested (at her insistence) and his sperm count was found to be drastically low.

Despite Todd's objections, and his near sterility, Emma used her Singer to sew a bonnet for her yet-to-be-conceived baby. She had made a wedding dress when her prospects for marriage were dismal, and thought to herself, "Heck, look how that had turned out."

Not long after completing the bonnet, yellow with light-pink trim, she took a pregnancy test and squealed at the results. When she broke the news to Todd, he was surprised, though not necessarily in a good way.

"Are you sure?" asked her husband, dumbfounded.

"Yes!" beamed Emma. She showed him the blue line on the over-the-counter stick.

Todd nodded dejectedly. "Honey, this is great news, I mean it. But I'm kind of worried about how we're going to afford having a kid."

Emma scowled at him. "We're bringing a baby into the world and all you can talk about is money?!"

Todd, knowing where the conversation was headed, apologized promptly and the couple spent the rest of the evening brainstorming baby names.

Nine months later, Emma gave birth to a beautiful baby girl, and their apartment, which seemed cramped before, became almost comical in its compactness. Their income, which they had to stretch immeasurably before the baby's arrival, was seriously insufficient as well. Emma felt the weight of their poverty daily in the TV dinners, her thrift shop clothes.

"Todd, Uncle Frank said he could put in a good word for you at Sküter & Simons, and I really think you should let him set up an interview."

"I don't know, Emma. Selling insurance? Do you really think I could cut it up there?"

"Of course you can. You're no idiot. You married me, remember?"

He smiled at the fact that she always got her way. He would go for the interview.

Emma was sewing Todd's jeans yet again, days before his office interview, when she had a revelation. She thought of her wedding dress and how Todd had proposed the day she completed it, of the bonnet and finding out she was pregnant after finishing that.

She wasn't superstitious by any means, but the coincidences seemed almost *too* fortuitous. What would happen if she sewed Todd a suit, maybe one more befitting a man with a cushy office job, a job that paid well and would get her out of the cramped apartment and into the sort of life which she and her daughter deserved? She purchased some silk fabric from a local store and began to sew a proper suit.

"Honey, you aren't going to believe this!" exclaimed Todd, rushing into his cramped kitchen. "I got the job!"

A colossal grin crossed Emma's face as she fed their daughter. "You did?!" Her eyes were immediately drawn to his brown business suit, which she had finished sewing just days before. Her plan had worked.

Todd struggled to learn the new trade—the right way to negotiate, when to follow up, when to close—but he was making sales and collecting checks twice the size of any he had made at the electric company. Emma was pleased in that regard.

With Todd's new job came new friends, social contacts, parties, and outings for the couple. They accepted every social invitation that came their way, and Emma developed a reputation around the office as the one to consult regarding party planning. She would stop in most afternoons for lunch, her baby on her hip, doling out freshly baked cookies and perky greetings to Todd's coworkers. She was better known around Sküter & Simons than her own husband.

It wasn't long before Emma and Todd were renting a quaint, three-bedroom house on the south side of Binghampton. With their daughter's first birthday approaching, they decided to celebrate both events with a big party at their new home. Friends, family, new neighbors, and co-workers were all invited. Emma exceeded their monthly budget on the soirée.

The house was alive the night of the party. Food, drink, and amusements both adult and childish were enjoyed by one and all. Todd and Emma's daughter had taken her first steps just days before and was making her way around the house in her mother's shadow. Emma formed new friendships and contacts, and cleverly felt out the social standings and occupations of all of her guests.

"Emma, dear, your antique sewing machine is precious!" exclaimed Mary Maplethorpe, pressing down on the pedal and watching the wheel spin. "My husband says you're known as quite the seamstress around the office."

"Yes, I really love the feel of the old machines," replied Emma, growing weary of Mary. Emma thought her a bore and her husband had only just started at Sküter & Simons. She was about to excuse herself to see to her other guests.

"An old friend of mine from college has a terminal cancer and we're holding an event to help with the medical costs. Would you be interested in sewing something to auction off?"

"Sure, of course," Emma said, not overtly enthused at the prospect.

"Excellent! It's going to be a formal ball on Groundhog Day at the Binghampton Country Club. I will make sure you and Todd get a formal invite."

Emma's ears perked up at "formal ball" and "Binghampton Country Club," two things that were sure to attract the local who's who. However, she knew that invitations to formal charity events often came with the expectation of a hefty donation. "We'd love to go. How much will the tickets cost? I feel silly asking, but we're running a little tight on money right now, with the new move and everything."

Mary laughed off her new acquaintance's worry. "It won't be a problem, Emma. If you make us something to auction, you'll get tickets at no cost."

The party was a great success. Emma told Todd excitedly about Mary Maplethorpe's charity ball and how they would be able to attend at basically no cost. Todd wasn't as thrilled to go, as he was under a significant amount of stress from the new move, the expense of the party, and his struggles to stay afloat at work.

Emma began sewing a ball gown for the upcoming charity event. She thought of it as her grand coming-out party, her entrance into a higher circle of society. She went to work madly, pouring her heart into the gown's design and execution. She had never before worked as hard or put as much of her being into something she had created.

She was frustrated when she had to pause in her great undertaking to give a half-day's effort toward an adequate quilt for the auction. Mary Maplethorpe was very pleased when Emma dropped it off. It was now only days before the event.

Todd came home each night that week looking sullener than the day before. He knew his time at Sküter & Simons was coming to an end; he just wasn't made for running numbers and the cutthroat world of sales. He tried to share his troubles with Emma, but she was so focused on their rising status that he did not want to derail her expectations.

"Todd, did you pick up the tux rental yet?"

"No. I'll get it tomorrow afternoon."

"Don't you think that's cutting it a bit close, dear? The ball is tomorrow evening." She had paused at her Singer to admonish her husband for his dour mood. "Everything is going great for us, Todd. Why do you look so depressed lately?"

"I'm just under a lot of stress, Emma."

"I know, honey. We both are. But things are working out for us. We'll be able to buy our own home sometime next year, and each step we take is going to be more stressful, but we have to keep at it. There's no going back, no dwelling on the struggle we've had, my love." Emma turned back to her task, and Todd walked off with his anxieties weighing heavier than ever.

The following afternoon Emma was putting the finishing touches on her grand ball gown. It had begun to snow and Todd walked through the door with his tux in hand, a light white dusting on his head and shoulders.

"It's supposed to get worse. I don't know how the roads are gonna be later."

"Oh, don't worry about that. It's a fundraiser for a dying woman; they'll have to hold it tonight. It'll be fine."

At six o'clock sharp their babysitter arrived from just down the road. Emma was finishing getting dressed while Todd fed the baby. She came into the kitchen in her elegant, navy-blue dress.

Todd looked up from the table. "You look stunning, Em. You are one fantastic dressmaker. You could be a pro."

"Thanks, honey. Now hurry up and get your tux on. I'll clean up the baby."

Todd's smile broke, knowing what he had to tell her next. "I've been looking outside every so often. It's getting pretty bad out. I'm sorry, I know how much you have your heart set on going, but we probably should stay home tonight."

Emma's face fell. She rarely showed any hint of anger, and she couldn't recall ever being genuinely mad at Todd, but the thought of missing out on an opportunity to rub shoulders with Binghampton's elite was too much to take. "Enough! We're going!"

Todd didn't respond but got up from the table and left the room. She was relieved, hoping he would hurry and get dressed so they would make it on time. However, Todd had only left to tell their babysitter they wouldn't be needing her services and to head home herself before the roads worsened. When Emma heard the front door close and found her husband sitting on the couch in the living room, still in his work clothes, she threw a fit.

The couple had the first nasty argument of their relationship that night. Todd stood up for himself and Emma was taken aback at his sudden defiance. She knew that she always got what she wanted from him, and this situation would be no different.

"The event's already begun, Todd. If you aren't going to drive me, I'll drive myself. I have no problem going alone."

Todd asked her not to leave. He was genuinely worried about the road conditions, in addition to his general displeasure with her words and actions of late. He had a terrible anxiety over his family's future and didn't need her driving off in her new ball gown into a growing nor'easter.

Emma ignored his pleas, put on her overcoat, and kissed her daughter goodnight. She was late and needed to hurry just to catch the tail-end of the auction. She jumped into their ten-year-old Honda, arranged her bulky dress, and backed out of the driveway and onto the road.

There was close to four inches in the street and the plows had only hit the major thoroughfares. Emma had some trouble; the front-wheel drive compact was slipping around the twists and turns as she came down the hill from their suburban neighborhood and toward the valley. Her dressy heels didn't make things easier, and the hem of her new gown kept catching her braking foot.

Meanwhile, at the charity ball, the auction had just ended. Mary Maplethorpe showed off the quilt that she had bid on successfully, which had been commented on by many a partygoer.

"Mary, who made that quilt again?"

"A really great gal named Emma Cowden. Our husbands work together at Sküter & Simons. I know it's unfashionable to bid on items at your own event, but I knew I had to have it when she brought it to me."

"Don't worry, dear. It really is a well-done piece. I would have bid higher myself if Randall hadn't cut me off," said Helen Vincent, the county supervisor's wife.

"Yes, there's certainly no etiquette issue, Mary," seconded Joy Petcosky, wife of the long-time city mayor. "You must get me in touch with her; I've interest in her work. It's a shame she couldn't make it. Blame the weather."

The upper-crust women were soon gathered up by their husbands and admonished for lagging behind when they should have been on their way, as word had spread that the roads in the hills were becoming nearly impassable.

Mary and John Maplethorpe were headed up home, when they spotted a tipped Honda in the ditch. Their 4x4 SUV cut the corners with little trouble and plowed through the constantly accumulating snow with little issue as John came to a halt near the wreck.

"Oh, my god, John; I think someone's lying out in the snow!" exclaimed Mary, as he jumped out of the car and rushed to the far side of the ditch.

He came upon a bloodied woman, her coat and navy-blue dress torn; fresh red streaks stained the decorative cloth. Mary hurried up behind him as he bent to check on the woman.

"She's not breathing. Jesus. She must have been thrown from the car." John tried to revive her to no avail.

Mary was on the phone with 911 when she got her first good look at the victim, and screamed. "Oh, God! That's Emma Cowden!" She was hysterical, and her husband had given up his fruitless attempts at resuscitation.

John took his wife back to the car and tried to calm her down. She was sitting in her seat, crying, when she spied Emma's quilt resting on her purse on the car floor. Mary grabbed the quilt and jumped out of the car, jogging back to Emma's lifeless corpse.

"Mary, what the heck are you doing?!"

She placed the elegant, finely crafted quilt over Emma and returned to the vehicle to wait for the ambulance. It covered her perfectly, almost as if it were sewn for that exact purpose.

MARTINUS' MANNEQUIN

"Marvel-ree!" exclaimed an old man in a heavy, flowing overcoat as he barged into the Curiosity Shop, unannounced, hauling a vintage retail display mannequin.

"What's this, Martinus?" asked Dr. Marvelry. "And you should know, better than most, it's pronounced 'Marvel-rye.'"

The new clerk, Drew, stood silently on a ladder attached to a bookcase, watching the scene unfold.

"The mannequin!" stated Martinus, as he placed it upright, with difficulty, against the shop counter. Its base was unsteady and it wouldn't stand on its own.

"I see."

"Dante is *in* the mannequin!" exclaimed Martinus, his eyes widening.

"I see."

"Ah, I knew you wouldn't understand..." said Martinus, wagging his finger at Marvelry. He pulled off his overcoat, revealing a wrinkled dress shirt and a shabby pair of corduroy pants, held up by suspenders. A large crystal pendant hung from a silver chain around his neck.

"Understand what, Martinus? What on earth do you mean, 'Dante is in the mannequin'? Dante Alfero?"

Martinus nodded in a frenzied manner. "Yes, our dear friend— the Illustrious Dante—has taken possession of this mannequin. He needs our help to gain his release so that he may explore the multiverse unimpeded!"

Marvelry looked over at Drew, who was staring at the interloper like he had just escaped from the Robertson Road Asylum. Drew, feeling uneasy, got down from the ladder and went to the storeroom.

"You've got to be joking, Martinus. I thought your obsession with the grimoires and astral projection nonsense was as far as you'd descend into fatuity. You're going to tell me that Dante has been in possession of this department store mannequin since his death?"

"I'm not entirely sure. But he has communicated with me from the spirit plane. He is trapped, Marvelry; do you not understand?"

"No, I've never understood your esoteric nonsense," said Marvelry. "Where did you find this thing?"

"I was working with a group of amateur paranormal investigators. We were at an old shopping center up north investigating a haunting, and I was using my spirit board to contact the dead. Dante made the mannequin move, and directed my pendant, spelling out my Christian name!"

"Anyone with a computer can find out your name and biography. You're a mildly successful author and occultist," said Marvelry, a slight grin lifting his lip.

Martinus didn't take offense at the light jab. "I made a deal with the property owner and took the mannequin home. Now, you might be wondering—how are we to know that it's possessed by Dante and not some other wayward soul? Well, I'll tell you. He knows things. Things about *you*, Marvel-ree. Personal things."

Marvelry didn't want to give credence to the fictions of an eccentric like Martinus, but part of him did (and always had) want to believe in the continuation of the living spirit beyond death. "Go on."

"I know you disapproved of my and Dante's investigations. What you so flippantly dismissed as 'paranormal fantasy.' *Ha.* It was no secret. But we were never satisfied, as you were, with simple illusions and parlor tricks. We wanted to know the deepest of truths, what lay beyond this world, the one illuminated by our best scientific minds."

Marvelry rolled his eyes.

"We were traveling on the Trans-Siberian Railway in search of the hidden cult of Rasputin, and discovered the indigenous shamans of Mongolia and Siberia—peoples with ancient traditions regarding communication with the spirit world during altered states of consciousness. Dante and I were amazed by their powers and wished to learn their secrets, so we studied with them for some time. Not long after, we travelled to Loreto in Peru, and drank cup after cup of Ayahuasca and learned the southern traditions, hoping that we might establish a connection with the dead."

Marvelry interjected: "As I recall, you two got high every day and stirred up so much trouble you were eventually deported by the Peruvian authorities."

Martinus shook his head and continued his monologue. "We did see things, visions of extra-dimensional beings. I believe that Dante learned something then, a knowledge which enabled him to *cheat death*. He longs to be free, to escape this endless series of possessions. Can you imagine how awful it must be? He has been working his way back to you. He seems to believe that *you* can help him escape the confines of the material world once and for all."

"Suppose I consider your ludicrous story. Why would Dante seek *me* out? I know very little of practical shamanism."

Martinus waved his hands and reached into his overcoat, removing and then unrolling his portable spirit board. He then undid his necklace and dangled the crystal pendant over the lettered mat. "Take it, Julian. See for yourself."

He grabbed the pendant from Martinus and held it above the board. "I'll humor you. Then once we're finished with this farce, you can leave."

Martinus closed his eyes, tilted his head to the ceiling, and held his arms aloft. He called out: "Is Dante Alfero present?"

Almost immediately, as if it were being maneuvered by a strong magnet below the board, the pendant directed itself from one letter to the next.

M......

A.......

Marvelry stared in disbelief as the pendant continued its route, stopping finally on the letter N.

M-A-N-I-K-I-N.

"I told you," said Martinus.

Marvelry flipped the board over, looking for a magnet, a false back perhaps—but nothing appeared out of the ordinary. "Good one, Martinus. I'm stumped. Is it some kind of remote-based trick? Let me see your palms."

He lifted Martinus' hands, and the older man shook him away. "It's no trick. I told you; Dante is in the mannequin. And he is literally spelling it out for us!"

"Okay, let me ask a question. Something personal." Marvelry held the pendant above the board again. "What was my father's first name?"

The pendant darted from one letter to another, this time more rapidly, before stopping on the letter L.

R-A-H-I-L.

"I don't understand, Martinus. Tell me how you're doing this. My father was known his whole life as Ralph Marvilynov, even on his legal and business documents. I'm not entirely certain that I ever told Dante his birth name either." Martinus shook his head, and Marvelry somehow knew he wasn't lying. They stared at the board, mystified.

Their contemplative moment was interrupted by Drew. "Sir, it's 3 o'clock, so I'm going to go drop off that sewing machine across town." He looked at the board, curiously. "What are you guys doing? Is that a Ouija board?"

"Yes, Drew. Martinus here is looking to sell it and he decided to give me a demonstration."

"Ok, cool. Those things are great. Well, I'll see you later," said Drew, shuffling away. He opened the door and turned back toward the men, curious what they were up to, before exiting the shop.

As soon as the door closed, Martinus excitedly turned his attention back to the board. "Marvelry! Now you see! It truly is Dante trapped in the mannequin. We must communicate further in order to help free him."

Marvelry, who had no patience for spiritualistic hogwash, suppressed his skepticism and held the pendant over the board again. He could come up with no rational explanation for what had transpired and was curious to see what would happen next.

"Good. Now let me lead," said Martinus. "Dante! How can we help you?"

The pendant swung quickly from one side of the board to the other, spelling out S-C-R-O-L-L.

"Scroll?" asked Martinus.

Marvelry shrugged.

"Dante, tell us, what do you mean by 'scroll'?"

Marvelry was startled by the force of the pendant, which spelled out T-R-U-N-K.

"I don't understand," said Martinus.

"Dante's trunk. I keep it out back. I've never really gone through it. I opened it briefly when I received it, but it gave me an ill feeling, and I haven't disturbed its contents since."

"Show me!"

Marvelry lead Martinus to the storeroom and pulled the trunk out from underneath a table. It made a scraping sound as they moved it over the floor. Marvelry opened the box and the heavy scent of incense permeated the air. The trunk was crammed full of various baubles and mystical objects: spell candles, a petrified bird's talon, Zoroastrian charts, Cascarilla powder. Marvelry was hesitant to remove the scroll, which lay atop a yellowed manuscript, so Martinus snatched it out.

They then returned to the front of the shop. Martinus unwound the lengthy scroll on the counter, next to the mannequin, and eagerly looked it over. "I can't believe he kept this from me," he mumbled. "Marvelry, the pendant, again!"

The pendant spelled out two words: H-Y-M-N. V-E-S-S-E-L.

Martinus searched the scroll for an ode or song, to no avail, while Marvelry stood over his shoulder. "I can't find it. There are spells, named witches, hexed animals and totems," said Martinus.

"Look," said Marvelry, pointing to an incantation: "'Necromancy Unto a Human Vessel.'"

"Necromancy! This is getting interesting. What could it mean?"

Marvelry gravely read the text of the spell. "This is for a reverse exorcism, in assisting a spirit in the habitation of a living being. But why would Dante want to possess someone? Something doesn't seem right."

Martinus lowered his voice. "This is taking a thorny turn. Maybe he wishes us to re-animate his body?"

"He was cremated and his ashes were spread over the Queehanna River. How would that work?"

"Oh. Right."

"Listen, I'm not entirely sure we're dealing with Dante," whispered Marvelry.

Martinus' enthusiasm seemed to subside. "There must be some misunderstanding..."

Marvelry turned to address the mannequin. "My dear instructor. For the life of me, I can't recall the first trick you taught me. I've been writing my memoirs and it seems a crucial detail worth recording. It wasn't the 'finger flash,' was it?"

"What is the point of this?" asked Martinus, skeptically.

The pendant dangled in Marvelry's hand, momentarily slack, and seemingly unsure. Eventually, it began moving over the board, spelling out F-I-R-E-B-R-E-A-T-H.

Marvelry grimaced. "Not quite, but the 'fire breath' certainly jogs the memory. Any sideshow performer worth his salt can learn to breathe fire in the first week of his tutelage." He lifted the scroll above an open hand and ignited the old parchment with a rod of fire from his palm. "Dante always said there was nothing more inelegant than a bearded woman with bulging cheeks and accelerant dripping from her mustache."

Martinus ran over to the scroll and stomped out the fire, but the portion dealing with necromantic practices was scorched black and illegible. "Why did you do that?!"

"The spirit of our dear friend isn't residing in that mannequin. 'Fire breath,' really?"

"But how can you be so sure? You don't—" Martinus stopped when he saw the pendant spinning wildly in Marvelry's hand. It then flew from his grasp and smashed into the wall.

"We must rid ourselves of that thing, immediately," said Marvelry.

Martinus shook his head. "I don't understand. If it's not Dante, who is it? And why would it lead me to you?"

Suddenly the overhead lights flickered and an apothecary bench slid across the floor, blocking the front door. It was followed by other sizeable pieces—an electric organ, a suit of armor, several bookshelves.

The two men raced toward the side door to escape but were blocked by a large covered cabinet which had moved several feet on its own. Their attempts to move it were futile, as it had taken on a supernatural weight, which no living man could overcome.

"Telekinesis! I have never witnessed such phenomena. Amazing!" exclaimed Martinus, breathing heavily.

"I have seen activity like this before, unfortunately. When I was traveling Eastern Europe after college—" said Marvelry. He was about to recount his experiences when a disembodied voice reverberated throughout the shop: "It took decades...but I found you, *Julian.*"

The pair was stunned by the voice, which seemed to originate from no place in particular. It was low and guttural, and the men could feel it in their chests. Marvelry recognized it instantly.

"What was that?" asked Martinus, mouth agape.

But the voice was only the beginning. The men watched as items throughout the shop began to levitate and propel toward them.

"Martinus, take cover!" Marvelry dove as a humidor struck Martinus, knocking him unconscious, then crawled underneath a table, narrowly evading a Native American hatchet axe, which struck the floor near his feet.

Like Dante and Martinus, Marvelry, too, had at one point investigated occult beliefs and practices. While traveling Europe in his early twenties, he crossed paths with a group of Slovakian Rosicrucians and watched them perform a séance in a small apartment. They had attempted to conjure Elizabeth Bathory, a Hungarian countess who killed hundreds of young women during her reign and is said to have bathed in blood. However, as an unforeseen result of their actions, a female member of the group acted as if possessed by a spirit of malcontent, one she came to describe and refer to as 'Belial.'

Objects moved in that small, dank apartment, seemingly of their own volition, while the woman howled and thrashed about. Marvelry had always considered the possibility that there were less than supernatural factors at play, as the candles that lit the room had conveniently dimmed during the action.

However, at the time, he accepted the situation for what it appeared to be (while maintaining the possibility of a hoax), and interpreted the possession as a diagnosable issue arising from the woman's own psyche. He directed his new associates to surround the woman with mirrors, as he had come to recall a psychiatry experiment with a woman exhibiting signs of multiple personality disorder. The clinician forced the patient to face her entire oeuvre of being head-on, to mixed results. Marvelry had learned of this treatment during his college years, where he had studied, participated in, and even directed psychological experiments.

After a series of failed attempts to address the young Slovak woman, he finally found the right arrangement for the mirrors, and was able to goad the possessed to delve into her demonic purpose.

The group looked on in amazement as the young traveler was able to coax their friend back to reality. From that point on, Marvelry became a firm believer in the psychical nature of what was most often deemed 'supernatural,' but he was finished with dabbling in occult practice himself—preferring to listen to the stories and study the associated relics, as opposed to bearing witness to the supposed events.

Marvelry left the country and hadn't thought of the incident in decades. Now, hearing the voice again, it seemed evident that the possession had been a truly mystical occurrence, and the demon, which he had managed to exorcise, sought revenge—specifically, against him.

"If this is Belial, I would advise you to reconsider," said Marvelry. "You don't realize the sorts of things you may be awakening in this shop."

The demon laughed and the table split over Marvelry's head. He rolled away from the falling debris and found cover behind a large rosewood headboard.

Marvelry watched as the slumping mannequin's plastic limbs became animated and the figure approached him, its inflexible feet clacking against the hardwood floor.

"Your mirror trick was clever, but I found other avenues." The terrible voice again emerged from no discernible location. "I've crossed land and sea, appropriated person and object alike, to find you."

The mannequin yanked the headboard out of the way and picked Marvelry up by his vest. Marvelry pushed back and his pursuer's stiff hands lost their grip, allowing him to escape.

The demonic force followed the aging magician through the maze-like rows of displaced furniture and broken objects, which now littered the floor. Items of every shape and size continued to crash around them, as Marvelry fought back against the awkward appendages of the dummy. Their brawl led them toward the side door, where they repeatedly knocked against the covered cabinet blocking the exit. The sheet which had been draped over it gradually fell to the ground from their cumulative impacts, revealing the formerly concealed item. It was Martinus' forgotten bureau and its appearance seemed a godsend to Marvelry.

He hadn't known what to do with the device after retrieving it from the dilettante magician the Great Maravelli at the benefit gone awry. He ended up burying it behind other items in his shop, concealing it, as he was unsure if he should risk attempting to destroy it. He knew that the bureau held a terrible, largely unknown power, and his ultimate fear at the time was unleashing it, despite his staunch skepticism.

Marvelry intended to stuff the mannequin into the bureau and utilize its disappearing mechanism, the same way he had dispatched the freshly risen corpse that threatened the benefit attendees. When he managed to push the troublesome being away, he flung open the doors to the bureau. But before he could make another move, the mannequin tackled him and they both tumbled inside.

He struggled to escape the small space, kicking and batting the mannequin's arms away, but he was pinned down. The possessed form attacked Marvelry viciously and choked him. He was starting to black out when the mannequin was suddenly yanked away, and Marvelry was freed from the being's death-grip. He looked out of the bureau to see Martinus struggling with the fiend.

Marvelry rolled out of the cabinet and yelled: "Martinus, toss it in!" He grabbed the legs of the mannequin, while Martinus controlled the torso, and the pair stuffed the demon inside of the bureau, slamming the doors shut against its flailing limbs. The cabinet rocked back and forth from the unholy force that raged inside. Before the demon could break out of its confines, Marvelry turned the door handles inward, engaging the mysterious mechanism that Martinus had designed. Immediately, the suspended objects fell to the floor, and the bureau stopped shaking. The shop became still.

Marvelry looked at Martinus and slowly opened the wooden cabinet. He breathed a sigh of relief to find nothing inside.

"I didn't know it could do that!" said Martinus, astonished.

"What? You built it!" replied Marvelry, incredulously.

"Well, not exactly..."

Marvelry sighed at the old mountebank. "Do you have any idea how to destroy this thing—without unleashing hell?"

The two were still discussing how to safely dispose of the bureau when Drew returned. He was shocked, to say the least, at the sight of the shop's chaotic state, and at Martinus and Marvelry, who looked like they had been in a ten-round boxing match. "Oh, wow. Do you guys need a minute?"

"A slight misunderstanding," said Marvelry, straightening his vest. "It's all sorted out now."

SIREN SONG

In the spring or summer, anyone coming or going from Building B at Mountain Shadows could hear the sounds of instruments from the open window of Nick Peak's apartment. He was struggling as a professional musician, and had become a regular at the pawn shops in town. As time passed the sounds of cello, upright bass, and electric organ had faded—to the veiled delight of his immediate neighbors—his acoustic guitar remaining his sole musical outlet. The only person who had ever let his complaints be known to Nick, regarding his choice of hobby, was Nap Fontaine, the curmudgeonly maintenance man, but he complained about everything and would continue to do so unto death.

It was one warm afternoon in late May, while Nick was strumming away at his Martin guitar, that the sounds of an electric organ could be heard from somewhere inside his building. Curious, he wandered the hall to discover the source of the experienced playing. The sound was originating from somewhere on his floor, and he went door to door, placing his ear against apartment 216, then apartment 215. Finally, it became clear that it was the unknown tenant in 214 which had brought new musical life to Mountain Shadows.

Stylistically, the piece reminded him of several different Romantic Era composers. The playing and composition were so exquisite he felt ashamed that he couldn't name it. Transfixed and unaware, Nick began to turn the doorknob. He had at many times been emotionally moved by music, but never had he seemingly lost control of his physical being.

Suddenly the music stopped and Nick could hear what sounded like a chair scraping the floor inside. Hesitant to disturb a fellow musician, and quite demure in his natural state, he hurried back to his apartment before the new tenant could discover him.

Back in his living room, high on adrenaline, Nick thought he could hear a door open and close down the hall. He paced around, excited by the prospect of an adept musical neighbor. For the rest of the afternoon, he contemplated how he might befriend the fellow musician, hoping to have somebody new with whom to play and compose.

Nick was returning home one evening from his job at Sardo's Cafe when he finally saw the inhabitant of apartment 214. An attractive young woman stepped out, and he paused to look at her. She was small, svelte, with shoulder-length auburn hair and thin lips; pretty but understated. She wore a blue dress and brown flats, and had an air about her that defied the dullness of the apartment complex.

"Hello," said Nick, nodding at her cordially. He realized he reeked of coffee beans and hoped she wouldn't notice.

"Hi," said the woman.

"Welcome to Mountain Shadows!" said Nick.

"Thank you." She smiled as she locked the door to her apartment, then walked in Nick's direction, toward the stairwell.

"I'm Nick." He raised his hand meekly, but didn't offer to shake, as to keep a comfortable distance for both of them.

"Brenda."

Before Nick could gather up the courage to ask about her organ playing, she passed him and descended the stairs. He sighed and went into his apartment to work on a new song.

Nick was in the basement laundry room that evening, folding his clothes, when Nap walked in, muttering something under his breath. He walked over to a dryer and removed quarters from the machine's coin box.

"This organ has got to stop. Even *you* must be sick of it by now," said Nap. Brenda's muffled playing could be heard through the vents and ducts.

"I don't mind it."

Nap rolled his eyes. "Day in and day out. This isn't a concert hall, ya know. People *live* here." Nick continued folding in silence, and Nap picked back up. "Ah, but why would it bother you? You're a fellow *music-maker*! Hah. At least I don't hear you playing the same thing 'round the clock."

Nick left the room as Nap continued to complain about Brenda's playing.

Nick continued to listen closely to the music coming from Brenda's apartment in the weeks following. It had a mournful quality that seemed to parallel his own lone existence. He found himself pausing in the hallway when coming and going, drawn to her door. She played continually, seemingly sunup to sundown. He heard a few restrained complaints on their floor, and near daily whinging from Nap, but for the most part, it seemed his neighbors either didn't notice, or didn't care, that Building B had its own Silent Era movie score.

Nick passed Brenda in the hallway several times over the following weeks but lacked the stomach to inquire about the organ or say anything beyond a simple hello. He ran into her one day after teaching a lesson, guitar case in hand, and hoped that would signal to her that he was a fellow musician. But she simply smiled and went into her apartment, and Nick kicked himself for not speaking up yet again. He had seen a few unfamiliar men enter her place recently, so he was sure she wasn't opposed to conversation, or company. From time to time, he would catch a neighbor loitering near her door, stopping and listening, seemingly fascinated by the woman and her organ.

One evening, his friend Brad, who lived on the floor below, came upstairs to play Magic: The Gathering. The two were in the middle of a heated game when they heard the organ music starting up down the hall.

"That's it, man," said Nick. "That's the girl I've been telling you about."

"She's pretty good," said Brad. "But what is she playing? It sounds like something out of a Hammer horror film."

"Beats me. That's the only kind of stuff she ever plays. It's dark, sure, but I think it's strangely...pretty."

Brad took off his Jets ball cap and playfully swatted at his pal. "Aww, how *sweet*. Haha. I wonder what else she's good at..." He smirked.

"Well, I've seen a few guys go in there already. You're probably too late."

"A few guys? And she's been here *how* long? Sounds like good odds to me."

When Brenda stopped playing for two days straight, it was hard not to notice. Nick started to miss the soft music; it had become an anodyne backdrop to his home life.

Nick was on the couch, tuning his guitar on the second night of Brenda's hiatus, when there was a light knock on his door. When he got up and looked through the peephole, he was stunned to see Brenda staring back at him. He quickly ran his hand through his hair and opened the door.

"Hi, Nick. I'm sorry to bother you," said Brenda.

"Hi! You're not bothering me at all. How are you?"

"I've heard you playing guitar. You're good. I was wondering if you knew anything about organs?"

Nick's face lit up. "Actually, I do. I had one for years. I only just sold it a few months back."

"Oh, good. Would you mind coming over and looking at mine? I'm having an issue with it."

"Not at all." Nick was excited to show off his musical knowledge, and hoped that the interaction could lead to something more.

"I'm hitting the keys and no sound is coming out," said Brenda as she led him into her apartment, which was exceptionally plain. The furniture was sparse and not a single picture hung from the cold, white walls.

"Mine used to do the same thing on occasion. I could probably—" Nick stopped when he saw the organ sitting in the corner of her living room. His eyes were drawn to a partially torn Deep Purple sticker next to the lower keyboard; the organ looked the same as when he had sold it to Dr. Marvelry.

"These problems tend to be electrical." Nick crouched and removed the rear panel, revealing various circuits and hanging wires. It didn't take him long to locate the loose connection. The organ's speaker started to hum softly. "Hit a key for me."

Brenda struck the Middle C and a rich tone emanated from the aging speaker. "I can't believe you fixed that so quickly. Thank you!"

Nick nodded. He decided not to reveal his past ownership of the instrument. "It's no big deal." He paused, nervously, thinking of something to say. "So, how long have you been playing?"

"Only a few years."

"I know you practice all the time, but you're really good for only playing a few years."

"Well, Brahms has been like therapy to me. I start playing one of his chorales and I get lost, and seem to lose time," said Brenda, dreamily.

They continued to chat about music, and Nick finally gathered the courage to ask her out, inviting her to dinner that night.

"Thank you for the invite, but not tonight," said Brenda, taking a seat in front of the organ. "If you don't mind, I really want to get back to my playing."

Downtrodden, Nick let himself out of the apartment, with one last look over his shoulder at the seemingly obsessed young woman before shutting the door. The organ came to life behind him, and Brenda's mellifluous outpouring was once again a part of his day-to-day.

Nick continued to enjoy Brenda's music but watched in disappointment as various men entered her apartment. He was especially disheartened when he saw her walking down the hall one day with Brad. He figured the pair must have hit it off, because his friend missed their weekly card game.

When his friend didn't respond to his texts the following week, Nick grew worried, as Brad had never been one to ignore his messages. Nick had his buddy's extra key and decided to check his apartment, hoping that Brad had lost his phone and had just been really busy.

Nick knocked, waited, then knocked again. When there was no answer, he unlocked the door.

He jumped back, startled, when Brad's cat, Zinger, jumped at him and ran around his

feet madly. When he followed Zinger into the kitchen, he was taken aback by the smell of rotting garbage. It was clear that Brad hadn't been home in a while.

When he left the apartment he was startled to see Nap standing in the hall, sneering.

"What are you doing in there?!" Nap demanded.

"I was looking for Brad. He's been gone for days," said Nick, stepping into the hall.

Nap eyed Nick's hand. "Residents aren't allowed to share keys. It's a violation of lease terms."

Nick was too concerned to get caught up in a petty argument with the man. "Have you seen Brad?"

"No. And I was about to check in there, myself. His apartment smells something awful. I've received a few complaints already. Damn it, if it's not rats or that goddamn organ music, it's something else." Nap walked into Brad's apartment and slammed the door. Nick could only think to check with the last person he had seen accompanying Brad. He went back upstairs to Brenda's apartment, where, as usual, she was playing her organ. He swallowed the lump in his throat and knocked firmly. The playing stopped; he heard the scrape of her chair, footsteps, and then Brenda appeared at the door.

"Brenda, have you seen Brad Harlec? He lives downstairs."

"Who?" she replied, looking genuinely confused and taken aback by his serious tone.

"Brad *Harlec*. I haven't seen him in a week or so, and I thought you knew him..."

"Come in, Nick."

He followed her inside, and described Brad in more detail, explaining that he thought he saw them together the week before.

"Oh, *Brad*. You haven't seen him? I ran into him in the parking lot the other night. He was arguing with the maintenance man," said Brenda.

"Nap?"

"I guess," replied Brenda. "Brad helped me carry in my groceries and I made him something to eat."

"I'm really worried. He's not picking up his phone or responding to my messages." It was then that Nick noticed what looked like Brad's favorite Jets cap hanging on the corner of the organ.

Brenda suddenly snaked her hand through Nick's arm and got oddly close, which rubbed him the wrong way. "Do you want to stay for dinner?" she asked.

He considered the invitation—he was finally getting a response out of her—but it didn't feel right, since he was searching for his friend. He looked back at the ball cap once more before mumbling a goodbye and hurrying out of the apartment.

Nick went to the local police station and spoke with a detective named Mohr. He was unsure of what he should be doing to find his friend, and he didn't have any of Brad's family contacts. The detective wrote up a report, took Nick's information, and assured him that he would look into Brad's disappearance.

That night Nick heard a commotion in the hallway and peered out of his peephole. Two uniformed policemen walked past his door, talking. He assumed they were going to speak to Brenda, because he had told the detective she was the last person he had seen with Brad. Nick stood in the vicinity of his door, strumming his guitar absentmindedly, listening for any more action out in the hall. Ten to fifteen minutes later he heard a door open and a few muffled goodbyes, so he looked out of his peephole and saw the cops pass again.

Nick was pacing his apartment when he heard a door open again and someone walking the hall. He spied Brenda walk past, and thought nothing of it until she turned and paused briefly at his door. The way she seemed to stare at his peephole in that brief moment before heading back down the hall made him shiver. He saw that she was irritated, and was glad she had decided not to confront him just then.

Days later, Detective Mohr called Nick and told him that Brad's family and employer had also recognized that he was missing, and that everyone was taking his disappearance seriously. While they were going over his usual haunts and hangouts, Nick reiterated that Brenda was the last person he had seen with Brad and that he was sure he had seen Brad's Jets cap in her apartment.

"We talked with Ms. Wells the other night, along with a few of your other neighbors. The problem with missing persons cases is folks' memories really aren't that great, so stories conflict about where and when people say they saw someone last," said Detective Mohr. "Know that we have an eye on Mountain Shadows, Mr. Peak. We are starting to piece things together on another missing persons case that also seems to be connected to that apartment complex."

Nick was dejected; it seemed like there had been no progress in finding Brad since he had notified the police. He sat in his apartment in near silence, the ever-present din of the organ in the background, and couldn't help but think that Brenda knew more than she was letting on. She was strange—not that it was weird that a young, attractive woman had a number of men coming to her apartment—but the fact that she might be so jaded they never stuck around for more than a night or afternoon.

Nick had the following day off from the cafe and no guitar lessons planned, so he decided to stop and see his pal at his preferred pawn shop.

"Hello, Nick. I'd say I'm glad to see you, but it seems like whenever I do, you're selling me a piece of yourself," greeted Dr. Marvelry, half-jokingly, as Nick entered his shop.

Nick chuckled. "I won't be pawning anything today. I'm actually hoping you might be able to shed some light on one of your customers."

"How can I be of service?"

Brad's missing persons case had made the local paper that morning. Marvelry had read the article, so Nick caught him up on his own involvement. "It's really a strange coincidence, how the organ ended up just down the hall from me," said Nick. "The woman's hiding something. I'm sure she knows more about where Brad went, or even who he was with when she last saw him. I spotted his cap in her apartment when we were talking and she started acting funny."

"I do remember her well; how could I forget? She played like a woman possessed when she tried out the organ in the store."

Nick was frustrated, and he felt he was just spinning his wheels. "I'm sorry. It was silly of me to come in and hope you'd have some special insight into this. It's really just a coincidence that we've both dealt with Brenda."

Marvelry paused, considering if he should share what he was thinking with the afflicted young man. "Well, since it was in the papers at one point—I guess I can speak of it," he said. "Brenda Wells was a victim herself, not too long ago. She was attacked with a knife in a cemetery in Lestershire and left for dead. We didn't delve into her history when she came in, but it was evident that she had moved to Binghampton to start over. The fact that she seems standoffish, impersonal, or just a little odd, is probably natural, given what she's experienced."

Nick agreed. He and Marvelry chatted a while longer, but he ultimately left with more questions than answers.

The organ music, which had been a strange yet calming presence in Nick's life, became a grim reminder of his friend's disappearance. While Dr. Marvelry's information about Brenda had made her seem pitiable to Nick, he planned on keeping his distance from her going forward. He had taken Zinger in while the authorities searched for Brad. Every day was tougher than the last, knowing that the longer his friend went missing, the more likely it was that he would be found dead.

Nick was leaving his apartment one morning to teach a guitar lesson across town, when he bumped into Brenda in the stairwell. She smiled at him as if they were old friends.

"Nick! You're just the guy I wanted to see."

"Hi," he said, leaving ample space between himself and Brenda.

"I'm having a new issue with my organ," she said, slinking toward him, invading what little personal space he had. "Can you come over and take a look at it again?"

Nick backed up into the railing. He was sure he had heard her playing during his breakfast. "Not right now. I've got to run."

"It'll only take a minute," Brenda said, twisting her hair between her fingers.

Had it been a few weeks prior, Nick would have leapt at Brenda's invitation, but his gut told him it wasn't worth it. "Sorry, maybe later," he said and hustled down the stairs and out the building.

When Nick returned in the early afternoon, he wasn't surprised to hear music coming from Brenda's room, but was taken aback by the style of play. She was hammering the keys with an undisciplined vigor, as if she *demanded* to be heard, the music's usual subtle elegance replaced by a maddening intensity. He heard Nap stomp down the hall and bang on her door, shouting at her to stop, but his demands did nothing to subdue Brenda's frenetic performance.

110

"I'm gonna go find my axe! If you're still playing when I get back, I'm gonna take it to your organ!" shouted Nap.

Nick was sitting on his couch, inattentively watching TV, when Zinger hopped up on the end table next to him and knocked his smartphone to the carpet. The screen lit up and Nick looked down to see he had missed a series of text messages. When he picked up his phone and swiped from the lock screen his heart leapt—the texts were all from Brad.

Hey, St. Nick! Jesus, my dad says they have the cops and everyone looking for me. I'm def not missing, buddy. I've been shacked up with this rich chick I met at the Tumble On Inn. Her family owns this sweet lake house in Lake Placid and we've been hiking, kayaking, partying. I prolly should've told you guys, but time flies…

Message two: *I've been meaning to quit that crap job anyway. Sorry for any trouble, pal. Will be back in town soon. We'll play cards, pool, drink some brew!*

Message three: *Shit! Zinger! Could you feed him, dude?*

Nick was laughing by the time he finished reading. *Goddamn Brad met a girl and went on an extended vacation. Lucky guy.* Nick messaged his friend back, congratulating him and asking for a picture of the young lady.

Nick could still hear the organ in the background, but Brenda's playing had lessened in intensity, regaining its calming influence. He felt elated, almost giddy, following the revelatory texts. That he could have believed a quiet woman who spent her days playing classical music may have had something to do with Brad's disappearance made Nick feel foolish. He had spent too many days cooped up in his apartment alone, he thought, and had let his imagination get the best of him. He felt bad for blowing her off earlier in the day.

After showering and putting on a nice pair of slacks, he walked down the hall and knocked on Brenda's door, anxious, but spirited.

The music stopped and the door opened. Brenda had an unsettled look about her. "Hello."

"Hi, Brenda. I'm sorry about earlier. I was feeling pretty upset about Brad, and I just wasn't in the mood to talk. He's fine, it turns out—he's just been out of town—but I feel crappy for not helping you with your organ."

"It's okay. It wasn't a major issue, and I think I figured it out," said Brenda. She paused. "But thanks."

"Well, I guess I'll see you later." He started to walk away, when Brenda called out to him.

"Hey, Nick?!"

He turned around. "Yeah?"

She smiled, curling her lip. "You wanna come in and watch TV or something?"

Nick followed her back inside. He was excited by the unknown and the possibility of any type of relationship with Brenda, and finally allowed himself to relax as he sat with her on her tiny sofa. They half-watched some network sitcom, but mostly chatted. Brenda was giving him a doe-eyed look, one he knew by instinct, and he made his move.

She accepted his kiss and they embraced passionately. Nick hadn't been with a woman in close to a year, and Brenda was more attractive than the typical girl he took home. He released all of his built-up anxieties on the couch with her.

"You're a great kisser," said Brenda, as they both attempted to catch their breath.

"We should've gotten together sooner," replied Nick, grinning.

She pushed him back on the couch and straddled him and they kissed some more. They were interrupted by a knock at the door. Brenda paused and said they should continue in her bedroom.

"Go ahead and get comfortable. I'll see who it is and tell them to go away," she said.

Nick strolled into Brenda's room confidently, excited by the evening's turn of events. He paused at how Spartan the room seemed. Like the living room, the walls weren't decorated; everything seemed fairly plain for the room of a young, artistic woman. Nothing caught his eye until he spotted a row of sneakers and shoes along the far wall that seemed too big to be Brenda's. When he bent down to investigate he was startled by a few more abrasive knocks at the front door.

Odd she hasn't gotten the door yet, Nick thought. He kicked his shoes aside and sat on the bed. The apartment was silent for a few brief moments, when a phone buzzed on the nightstand. He saw the lock screen flash and did a double-take when he caught sight of a picture of Zinger.

Nick leapt off the bed and picked up the phone. He saw the beginning of his congratulatory message to Brad and knew for sure it was his friend's phone. He dropped the phone when the knocking at the front door became an insistent pounding. When Nick turned, Brenda was approaching him with a long knife of some sort, but he couldn't process much, as she was already plunging it into the meat of his shoulder.

He screamed and tried to push her away, cutting his hands on the serrated blade. Brenda lunged at him, but he managed to slip away from her along the wall, using his own blood as lubricant. He noted a completely vacant look in her eyes, something animalistic and utterly inhuman.

Nick managed to kick Brenda in the stomach, and she collapsed to the rug, allowing him to flee out of her room and into the hallway.

"Help! Help!" screamed Nick as he stumbled away from his attacker. There were repeated thuds against the front door; it sounded like someone was trying to break in. He made his way out into the living room, Brenda chasing down the hall after him.

The front door cracked open in the frame as Brenda plunged her knife into Nick's back. He stumbled forward and twisted supine onto his old organ. Blood gushed from his wounds and over the white keys as the speaker blared a dozen cacophonous tones. Nick's last vision in life was that of Brenda looking him dead in the eye, slitting his throat from ear to ear. Her eyes burned with a callous disregard.

Nap and a plainclothes policeman rushed into the room, tackling Brenda—but it was too late for Nick. He died in the ambulance on the way to the hospital. He had lost too much blood.

An article in the *Sun Press* quoted Detective Mohr, lauding Nick's part in the pursuit and capture of the Mountain Shadows serial killer. "Mr. Peak immediately recognized that there was a connection between Ms. Wells and Brad Harlec's disappearance. It was at his insistence that we assigned a regular patrol to the complex. When Mountain Shadows custodian, Nap Fontaine, stumbled upon Ms. Wells' disposal area, he quickly notified our officer, having seen many of these men with Ms. Wells, and led him to her apartment. If Nick hadn't come to us with his information and kept up his inquiries around town, he, too, might have disappeared like those other men, in that deep drainage pipe in the woods—and a killer would still be loose in our community."

THE NEW ASSISTANT

"So, how'd we do today?" Dr. Marvelry asked the new clerk, Drew, who stood at the register, counting his drawer.

"Pretty good, sir," replied Drew. He went over the day's receipts with the shopkeeper, who listened approvingly. Marvelry was impressed that his new hire has been able to sell a *Chiller* arcade cabinet that had been gathering dust in a corner of the store for over a decade.

Drew was an anthropology student at Binghampton College and had been a regular customer of the Curiosity Shop, stopping in every so often to purchase magic books and tricks. He and Marvelry would have long conversations regarding local and regional legends. Marvelry saw him as a fellow adventurer, another seeker of the strange and mysterious. So when he heard Drew was in need of a job, it was an easy hire. Drew proved himself to be trustworthy, hardworking, and able to handle the job's many demands with ease (haggling with antique collectors requires a calm, unflinching disposition).

"Excellent. Now listen, I've a matter to attend to in Colonie tomorrow. A collector called and told me he owns a chastity garment that once belonged to Shaker founder Ann Lee." Drew nodded, unfamiliar with the name or religious sect. "It's not often that one gets to obtain the underwear of a resurrected Christ." Marvelry paused for a quick chuckle, before finishing his thought. "It's about three hours away, so it's going to take me most of the day to drive there, obtain the item, and get home. I'm going to leave the store entirely to you. Are you alright with that?"

"Yeah, sounds fine."

Before the two parted for the night, the shopkeeper reminded Drew of one important detail. "Keep in mind what I told you about some of the store's more *curious* objects. Some things are better left undisturbed."

Drew nodded. "Yes, sir."

"Well, have a good day tomorrow. I'll be back around 5 o'clock."

Drew's first day manning the shop alone started off relatively low-key. He sold a few hundred dollars' worth of merchandise—a raccoon skull, postcards depicting classic American freak shows, and a pregnant Japanese doll that birthed oddly shaped babies.

There was a lull around 2 p.m. and Drew found himself growing bored waiting around for the next person to walk through the door. He pulled out his copy of *Upstate Folklore Reader*, but not even fantastic tales of haunted trains and vanishing hitchhikers could hold his interest.

When no one had walked in for nearly two hours, Drew became restless. He wandered about, dusting, tidying up, trying to make the time pass. He ambled around the storeroom, searching through unsorted pieces that had either just come in or had never made it to the sales floor. He was about to leave the room when he noticed a large, black chest tucked beneath a table in the far corner of the room. The words THE ILLUSTRIOUS DANTE were stenciled on the side in big, white letters.

Drew thought back to what Marvelry had told him about Dante—how the magician had left him high and dry in Idaho, to travel the world with the occultist Martinus in search of transcendental experiences. Drew knew from his anthropological studies that some objects were believed to be imprinted on by conjurers, and that they should be handled with great care, and respect for the unknown. He was wary of hexed objects, even though he wasn't a tried-and-true believer in 'real' magic. Marvelry had told him enough of Martinus and Dante to know that the pair *were* believers.

Drew walked away from the chest and dusted another table nearby. He didn't want to defy his boss' wishes and muck about in things that had nothing to do with his job. But he kept glancing back at the chest. *What harm could it do to open it?* he thought.

He pulled the chest out from underneath the table, carefully, so as not to disturb any of the other items nearby and clue Marvelry in to his deed. He pressed his thumbs against the gold latches and heard a click from within. Slowly, he opened the lid to inspect the contents.

The inside smelled strongly of oak and coriander. Various items were scattered about, as if the last person to open the chest had closed it in a mad hurry. Drew pulled out a book labeled *Manual for Thelemic Magick* and immediately dropped it back inside, remembering Marvelry's warning. He dug through the chest and picked up a chicken foot totem. Again, he put it aside, avoiding any item which might have some type of ill supernatural effect. These items were clearly intended for occult practice, and he wasn't going to have anything to do with them.

Buried at the bottom of the chest was another book. It was bound shoddily and bore a nondescript, black cover. Drew opened the text and found the title page: *Anatomy of Occult Practice.* Underneath, the byline read: "Written by H.G. Wells."

Is this for real? thought Drew, flipping through the book. He looked up the title on his phone but found no mention of it anywhere. *Perhaps it's unpublished?*

Curious, and thinking that he might be holding a one-of-a-kind manuscript by one of the world's most famous authors, the type of item that would fetch a hefty price at auction, he sat down and read the introduction.

In recent years, it has come to my attention that there has yet to be an accounting of the fantastic bounty of para-scientific theory, spiritualist legend, and pagan ritual that has emerged from the Continent and New World, coinciding with the revolutions in technology and industry. This present text seeks to describe and detail what was once denigrated as witchcraft by the Authority, and therefore passed over in silence. Now in a more civilized age, enlightened minds have the freedom and ability to give the preternatural happenings proper study…

Drew skimmed the introductory pages, and again the manuscript was attributed to Herbert George Wells, in the year 1909. He had read a few Wellsian classics as a teenager—*The Time Machine, The War of the Worlds*—but this tome was more akin to a reference book than a work of fantasy fiction. He scanned the table of contents, intrigued by the chapters offered: Necromancy, Witchcraft, Summoning Spirits, Possession, Exorcism, and more obscure and unfamiliar mystical notions.

He opened up to the chapter on witchcraft, as he had recently been researching a local witch legend.

…the forests of the Catskills of New York State in America seemed to acknowledge the changes, exhibiting familiar sounds, odors, even behaviours regarding the early Dutch farmers' incursion. Their legends and tales were reminiscent of the mythic character of the Low Country from whence they emigrated. So when malady or sickness came upon family, crop, or cattle, the settlers could burn nearby oak groves and mitigate the power of the witte wieven. Oddly enough, it never occurred to the early Dutch emigres precisely why the forest witches of the Netherlands had concurrently chosen to make the voyage across the sea, and take up residence in the forests of the New World.

Drew had explored the woods of the nearby town of Oxford with his friends a week before to investigate a witch by the name of Helena Black. Thoughts of the journey flooded back to him—the wind blowing through the deciduous trees, the sour smell of dirt and fallen leaves, the creaking branches. He felt as if there was something sentient about the forest at that time, despite his ardent skepticism.

He dropped the book when he heard an indeterminate buzzing, seemingly from within the room. He thought, perhaps, somebody was doing construction work in the building over. He walked to each corner of the room, listening for the source, looking for an open vent. But the more he concentrated the more the sound dimmed, until it became nearly incomprehensible.

While maneuvering around boxes and unsorted antiques, a pair of handcuffs caught his eye and he retrieved them. Drew flipped them around, feeling the thick stocks and complicated mechanisms, meant to foil all but the double-jointed—they resembled the sort he had seen in promotional photographs of Houdini.

"Shit..." said Drew as one of the cuffs accidentally linked around his wrist. He returned to the box he had found them in to look for a key, but had no luck. He quickly gave up on trying to break out of them, as he was no magician, and resigned himself to just let them dangle from his wrist.

He returned to Dante's chest, still curious about the manuscript and sure it must be worth a great deal of money if it was, in fact, authentic. He picked up the book and leafed through, reading an account of a man driven mad by the bell of an antique clock.

...the rational belief being that the wretched terror young Mr. Donovan endured in his final hours had imprinted on the grandfather clock, nesting within the toll at each hour, compounding Mr. Worley's anxieties, and ultimately leading to his own family's demise.

Drew was startled from the paranormal account when a heavy sign abruptly fell against the storeroom door, shutting it. He paused, looking around the room, growing mildly anxious from the rush of adrenaline that accompanied the light shock.

Curious, he put aside the book and went to the door. But when he turned the handle, it had locked. *What the hell?* he thought. He tried turning the knob both ways, leaning into it, giving the door a few swift kicks—but the thing wouldn't budge.

Nervously, he paced in front of the door, thinking maybe he should just look for a screwdriver and undo the hinges. He knew it was a bad idea to leave a store empty on Clinton Street for too long; there was a seedier element that passed by now and then, sometimes even popping in, looking for a small item they could lift and quickly make off with.

Drew knocked his fist against a large dresser out of frustration, and his dangling handcuff caught on one of the brass handles. "No fucking way!" It was a one-in-a-million shot, locking on the last catch. He tried to manipulate the cuff loop, to no avail. With an exasperated howl, he yanked his arm away and the dresser drawer came flying out and onto the floor with a loud thud.

He knelt down to alleviate the pressure from the cuff, which was cutting into his wrist, and spotted a dozen formaldehyde-filled jars rolling around in the drawer. The jars clinked together as he picked it up, and he quivered when he realized that they contained the bloated corpses of fetal pigs. He studied them in their grotesque, almost-human stasis. One of the fetuses seemed to open and close its eyes. Drew yelped, jumping back and dropping the drawer to the floor, falling with it. The jars rattled and clanged against each other before rolling out onto the floor.

Drew broke down. He felt as if all the oxygen had been sucked out of the room, and he took in long, stuttering breaths to compensate. His mouth felt unbearably dry and large beads of sweat ran down his shaking face. Lightheaded and nauseous, he slumped to the floor.

Despite the generous size of the storeroom, Drew suddenly felt as if the walls were only a few feet apart. It was the same sense of unthinkable dread he had experienced as a boy when his father would lock him in the dark of the basement pantry for hours. He paced around anxiously, the drawer dragging along the floor beneath him. Remembering what his therapist had instructed him to do during a panic attack, he stopped attempted to relax, from head to toe. He returned to the Wells manuscript, hoping his curiosity would distract him from his predicament.

The section entitled Attached Spirits and Residual Hauntings intrigued him. He turned to the chapter and read an account of a woman who had been followed home by a spirit not long after dabbling in occult practice—casting charms and making talismans.

...the reckoning in her own parlor days later, for the mal entity had connected with Ms. Kipnis during the séance and had no need for a formal invitation. The erroneous belief that her home was inhabited by the ghoul, and not her person, led the madam to barricade herself in her root cellar, where she was found months later, long perished.

It was chilling to Drew, thinking about all of the legend trips he'd taken and haunts he'd explored, trying to catch a glimpse of something paranormal. He wondered, had some *thing* ever followed him home? It was only the week prior that he had tried to summon the malevolent spirit of a witch.

He and his friends had found the tree covered in x's near the old stone foundation off of Bowman Road, and he carved his three x's. Of course, no witch emerged, and his pals laughed at him for even attempting to test the myth. It was only now that he realized he had overlooked an important element of the ritual. One was supposed to carve the three x's and *then* ask Helena Black to perform some kind of heinous act. Drew wasn't looking for the bad karma that came with participating in something like that, so he had refrained from making his own morbid request.

Now he was considering his current plight and the possibility that there was more to the legend than he or most knew. What if Helena had attached herself to him precisely because he had summoned her and had not asked her to perform a task for him? By now, he knew the happenings in the room were informed, in some way, by what he read in the manuscript. Realizing he did not have the time to solve that mystery, he looked through the book for an answer.

Meanwhile, the strange buzzing had returned, and Drew's hand shook as he located a passage that seemed to deal with the removal of spectral possession. His trembling intensified when more mysterious sounds joined the phantom chorus—he heard the rattle of nails, the swift *shink* of sharpening blades, footsteps on the creaking wood floor. He looked up, completely taken aback when he saw a diagonal cut being made on the storeroom door, as if an invisible hand were digging a blade into the wood. Then another line cut across the first, forming an X.

X's, thought Drew. *Just like the woods.*

The disembodied footsteps shuffled closer. He searched desperately for their origin, but no one and nothing approached. His heart rate spiked when he felt something unseen push against his chest and release, and he heard a low voice call out his name.

Drew!

But it wasn't some cackling hag, nor a wailing specter. In fact, he knew the voice well, but that didn't make it any less terrifying. Its oppressive nature had not diminished, despite the fact that the man behind it had been buried four years prior.

C'mere, you little shit.

Drew recoiled, expecting his father's meaty fist to land square in his gut. He could smell his old man's cheap, woody cologne, and it took him back to a time in childhood he would just as soon forget.

Frantically trying to push the looming menace out of mind, Drew read through the passage.

...believing a spirit had attached itself to Ms. Rigby while she cared for the possessions of the Lord Harrison's recently deceased wife. The reverend clipped a lock of the parlour maid's hair and placed it in a bowl. With a small pin, he pricked her little finger and squeezed three drops of blood into the smouldering charcoal and myrrh. The Lord restrained poor Ms. Rigby, who flailed uncontrollably. The reverend made an entreaty to the attached spirit, that it let Ms. Rigby go. Fortunately, for the master of the household, the spell worked and the spirit left the parlour maid's body.

The stench of beer and cigarettes became all-consuming, tearing Drew from his reading. His father's voice shouted: *You want to spend another day in the basement?!* and the shop came to life. The smell of wood and paint joined the other foul odors, accompanied by a pronounced screeching.

Drew called out to the witch and implored her to free him, his voice wavering. "I summon you, Ms. Black, to destroy the door that confines me to this room; here I am a prisoner, as you were, trapped in your home by your neighbors while they burned it to the ground!"

In an instant, the clamor and all other spectral phenomena ceased. Drew investigated the door, and the X's had disappeared, as well. But the door was still locked. He leaned back against it, sighing, and caught sight of a key which was hanging on a hook obscured by the dresser. He grabbed the key and returned to the door, unlocking it, to his great relief. With his still-cuffed hand, he picked up the drawer and walked out to the front of the shop.

Dr. Marvelry returned from his trip not long after, having successfully purchased the Shaker heirloom. He held up the chastity belt as he greeted Drew. "I paid more than I wanted to, but it'll be a fine addition to my personal collection of spiritual undergarments," said Marvelry. "So, how did your day go, Drew?"

Drew stood stoically behind the counter and lifted his arm, revealing that his hand was still cuffed to the dresser drawer. Marvelry approached the young man and easily undid the loop. Drew sheepishly thanked his boss while he rubbed his raw wrist.

"Dr. Marvelry, I think there might be an unpublished manuscript out back. I couldn't find any reference to it online. It says it's by H.G. Wells. Do you know if it's one of a kind?"

Marvelry chuckled and shook his head playfully. "No, no. That's just one of Martinus and Dante's many frauds. A complete fabrication."

"Oh," said Drew, perplexed by what had transpired in the back of the store, seemingly spurred on by his interaction with the book.

Marvelry walked to the storeroom, but stopped and turned back to Drew. "The publishers laughed at them. As if anyone would be foolish enough to take the contents of that book seriously." He grinned and shut the door behind him.

GRAND ILLUSIONS

"Welcome to Sundown!" said world-renowned illusionist Nick Nickleby as he descended the front steps of his lakeside mansion to greet his guests. Nick had finally quit the road and had invited a host of magicians and close friends for a weekend-long retirement party.

"Nick!" said Dr. Marvelry, setting down his suitcase and embracing his former tour mate.

"It's been too long, Julian," said Nick, smiling warmly. He was in his late 50s, with dyed, jet-black hair and an angular face. Despite his age, he was very fit, and still quite attractive.

Marvelry introduced his assistant, who was carrying a few bags from his Cadillac. "This is Drew Hysell. He works for me. He's a big fan of yours."

"Pleased to meet you, Drew. A big fan, eh?" Nick chuckled.

"It's an honor, sir," mumbled Drew, who couldn't believe he was actually meeting the creator of the famous Nickleby Exchange.

"That's very flattering. But I'm no big deal; you already know the world's *greatest* illusionist," said Nick. "My tricks were made for TV."

"I've been retired for decades now, Nick. That title has been yours for some time," said Marvelry.

"How gracious of you," said Nick. He led Marvelry and Drew into the house and down a long hallway with polished wood floors and oriental rugs. The ceilings in most of the rooms were breathtakingly high. Impressionistic oil paintings lined the walls. They passed through what appeared to be Nick's living room, and were in awe of a series of large stained-glass windows depicting resurrections—those of Jesus, Lazarus, the Egyptian god Horus, and several other legendary figures.

"This is quite a place you have here. You've done well for yourself," said Marvelry. "Was this a monastery?"

"It's an historic estate with a *colorful* history," replied Nick, as he led them up a grand staircase. "I'll tell you more about it tonight."

He showed the men to their rooms, which were as luxurious as the rest of the home. Both featured four-poster canopy beds with ornate carvings and large, brass crucifixes.

They unpacked their belongings, dressed for dinner, then went down to the dining room, where a group of older men and an attractive woman were carrying on an animated conversation at the table, and passing around a bottle of wine. Everyone took notice of Marvelry's entrance, and he was greeted with smiles.

Two of the gentlemen got up and approached Marvelry. Though he had not seen them since the late-Eighties, he instantly recognized the pair, recalling their stage names: The Mysterious Drood and The Fabulous Barnaby.

"Julian, I'm so happy you could make it!" said Barnaby, who was already inebriated. He was the eldest of the magicians in attendance, but still spry and possessed of the manic energy which had captivated audiences in the '60s and '70s.

"Yes. A pleasure," said Drood, dryly. He was an exceptionally large man—built more like a linebacker than a conjurer. His trademark black mane had taken on a more skunk-like presentation as he aged, greying more on the top than anywhere else. "How's that *pawn* shop of yours?"

"It's good to see you both," said Marvelry, who was, in fact, displeased to see the pair—the drunkard Barnaby and the sourpuss Drood.

Everyone took their seats, Nick at the head of the long dinner table, next to his girlfriend, Claudia—a stunning redhead, not quite forty, and his former stage assistant. "Thank you so much for coming. You have all played an important role in my career, and I thought it appropriate to have you here as I bid *adieu* to the world of performance art."

The guests applauded and, as they ate, Nick recounted some of his finest moments as a touring magician. How he had headlined his first show in Chicago as a teenager. The internationally televised disappearance of the Taj Mahal in the mid-Eighties. His "burial at sea" in the late-Nineties. A four-year residency at the Pharaoh's Serpent Hotel in Las Vegas. Lastly, how he had been the one to introduce Marvelry's act to a national audience, and the joy he had experienced in seeing his friend reach unparalleled heights of international renown.

After he was done regaling his guests with food and story, Nick gave each a gift in gratitude for their support throughout his career. Barnaby received a flask once owned by Liberace. Drood got a leather case for his throwing knives.

Marvelry opened his box to reveal a silver, diamond-studded watch. Included with it was a note that read: *"For all the times we shared. May each hour be a reminder."*

He thanked Nick, who smiled. "It belonged to Howard Thurston. It was given to him by his mentor, Harry Kellar, upon his own retirement from the stage. It's the least I could do for a friend and illusionist of your caliber."

Barnaby exclaimed how fantastic a gift the watch was, while Drood looked enviously at Marvelry's much-more meaningful, and expensive, present. "Can I see it?" asked Drood. Marvelry handed the watch over. Drood inspected it, seemingly gauging its authenticity, while the other celebrants toasted their host and one other.

Nick concluded the evening's festivities by giving his guests a brief history of the mansion. He explained how the house had been inhabited by a religious cult, led by a zealot who called himself Malthus the Prophet. Members of the cult had engaged in horrible, depraved acts—blood sacrifices, cannibalism. The cult resided in the mansion, which they called Sundown, for a decade, until Malthus poisoned one of the group's more prominent members, drawing the attention of law enforcement. Malthus was hung for his crimes, and the rest of the cult faded back into society.

Everyone at the table was aghast at what they had heard. Marvelry, who felt light-headed from what he assumed was one too many glasses of wine, said goodnight to the revelers, and he and Drew retired to their respective rooms.

Breakfast was served at 9 a.m. the next day. Drew was surprised when the ever-punctual Marvelry showed up at twenty past the hour.

"Pardon me for my tardiness," said Marvelry, who appeared tired and somewhat sickly. He was wearing his expensive new watch. "I may have overindulged last night."

"No need to apologize, Julian," said Nick. "I'm happy you had a good time."

"Men our age shouldn't drink like that. You'll get sick—or worse," said Drood, coldly.

"You only drank two glasses of wine," Drew whispered to Marvelry. "Are you sure you're not coming down with something?"

"Maybe it was the cake and cigar, then. I'm sure I'll be alright."

Following the meal, Nick invited Marvelry, Drew, Barnaby and Drood out for a game of tennis. Marvelry, who still felt ill, sat on the sidelines while the four men took the court: Barnaby and Drood versus Nick and Drew. The two older magicians couldn't keep up with Nick, who practiced every day, and Drew, who was a fit, young man. Drood, making up for his lack of mobility, whacked the balls as hard as he could, some coming within inches of where Marvelry sat in the grass. Despite complaints from Nick to watch his form, Drood hit one ball directly at Marvelry, striking him in the chest. Marvelry crumpled over onto the clay court.

"Dr. Marvelry, are you okay?!" yelled Drew, running over to him.

"I'm okay," said Marvelry, attempting to push himself up from the ground.

Nick held out his hand for support. "Julian, you don't look well. Are you sure you're not ill?"

Marvelry shrugged. "I can't say. What I do know is that I should probably lie down." He excused himself from the rest of the group and returned to his room.

The tennis match soon ended and the remaining quartet returned to the mansion. Barnaby and Drood headed to the billiard room while Nick escorted Drew to the lower level to show off his art and antiquities collection.

"You're going to love this," said Nick. Their footsteps echoed as they walked along the damp, stone floor. They stopped in front of a massive wooden door, which Nick opened to reveal a vast room lit by candlelight. Inside were oddities of every shape and size, more macabre than anything Marvelry sold in his shop. Unwrapped mummies. Medieval torture devices. Shrunken heads. Ghastly paintings depicting witches at black masses feasting on children.

Drew didn't know what to say. "Nick. This is…"

"Fascinating, huh?" replied Nick. "Like Dr. Marvelry, my lifestyle has provided me with a means with which to acquire strange items from around the world."

Drew looked curiously around the room, bristling at the sight of a large doll with a devilishly painted face. Next to it was an apothecary bench, on which lay a mortar and pestle, which Nick claimed once belonged to Sir Isaac Newton. A few purple flower petals sat in the bowl.

"These things look like they can still do some damage," said Drew, examining a series of glistening bone saws that hung from the wall above the bench, each emblazoned with a pentagram.

"Those actually belonged to the Sundown cult. I've researched and purchased quite a bit of their furniture, books, and accoutrements." Nick opened a steamer trunk and dug out a shimmering purple robe with a blood-bespattered white cross stitched to the front. "And this was Malthus' sacrificial robe. The county historian believes nearly a dozen of his followers were killed in this house."

The tour was interrupted by Nick's phone. "I'm sorry, Drew. I have to take this. Feel free to explore the house."

Nick dropped the robe back in the trunk and hurried upstairs. Drew continued to look over the occult memorabilia, thinking back to the strange items he had seen and even interacted with over the past few months he had worked at Marvelry's shop. Nick's room was much darker in tone, the artifacts more menacing; he didn't want to be by himself down there for too long.

He wandered back up to the first and then second floor, peering into rooms, checking out the library, before he turned a hallway corner and ran into Nick's girlfriend, Claudia, who was red-faced and teary-eyed.

"Excuse me," said Drew.

"Oh, I'm sorry for bumping into you like that."

"Are you alright?"

Claudia, realizing how she must have looked, wiped her eyes. "Yes, I'm fine. It's *Nick* who has the problem."

"What's the matter?" asked Drew, hesitatingly. He had little experience dealing with adult women.

"He's a sociopath, to put it bluntly. It's like he has no regard for me or anybody else. Selfish bastard."

Drew couldn't believe that she was telling him these things. "Nick? Really?"

Claudia smirked. "Yes, the great Nick Nickleby."

"I'm sorry to hear that, Claudia."

She made move to leave, then paused, looking him over and smiling conspiratorially. "Nick's shown you his collection. You should come up and see some of *my* stuff."

Drew blushed; he was unsure of how to react to a beautiful, mature woman seemingly inviting him to her room. "I shouldn't, Claudia. Nick's been great to me and Dr. Marvelry…"

She laughed. "Maybe some other time." Drew took a step to leave and she stopped him. "He's a master of deception, on and off stage, kid. Don't let him fool you." She then walked off, leaving Drew to question Nick's integrity. He wanted to give his hero the benefit of the doubt, but Claudia's tears had been very convincing.

Hoping to avoid any more awkward run-ins, Drew went back outside for a relaxing walk around the property. There was a large garden adjacent to the house, and he wandered up and down its many rows, soaking up the sights and smells. The solitude was welcome after hours of interaction with such eccentric personalities.

Nick's estate was extravagant. The premises were well-manicured, and all around was green and lush with life. Marvelry may have been the more celebrated magician, but Nick certainly lived the more luxurious lifestyle.

There was a maze of well-trimmed hedges, a multitude of blossoming fruit bushes, and countless variety of exotic plants. He came upon a bed of purple, hooded flowers and crouched to get a closer look. He tumbled backward when he heard someone shout, "Stop!"

He turned to see Barnaby hurrying toward him, waving his arms.

"Don't touch those," said Barnaby. "They're poisonous!"

"Poisonous?"

Barnaby nodded, then helped Drew to his feet. "Highly poisonous. Wolfsbane. Drood and I were out for a walk yesterday afternoon and he warned me about those. He's an expert in herbs and medicines."

"Wow, I'm glad you told me," said Drew, relieved. He walked with Barnaby to the end of the row as they chatted.

"I'm sorry to hear Marvelry isn't feeling well. It's a shame. This is really some estate, so much to take in and enjoy."

"Yeah, I don't know what's up with him," said Drew.

"We go way back, Marvelry and me. I actually knew him before I met Nick. We had a mutual friend in Dante Alfero…"

"The Illustrious Dante?!" asked Drew, thinking back to his experience with the conjurer's phony grimoire.

"That's right," replied Barnaby. "Marvelry was just a young man when we met. Not much older than yourself, though not half as...fit." He looked Drew up and down then smiled.

Drew laughed uncomfortably. "I should probably go check on him, actually. He might need something."

"Oh, please send my regards."

"Sure," said Drew, starting to walk away.

"Well, it was nice to talk to you, Drew. I hope we can spend more time together before the weekend is through."

When Drew got back to Marvelry's room, he found his boss in rough shape. The older man was struggling to breathe. Drew rushed over to the bed. "Dr. Marvelry! "Are you alright?"

Marvelry licked his lips and strained to speak. "My stomach is burning."

"We need to take you to a doctor."

"No, no. Just help me take off this shirt. I'm very warm."

Drew assisted Marvelry in sitting up and removing his undershirt. In the process, Marvelry's watch was nudged out of place, briefly revealing a small mark on his wrist, which caught Drew's eye and piqued his curiosity.

"Dr. Marvelry, can you take your watch off?"

Marvelry slid the timepiece from his wrist to reveal a large, red blotch on his skin.

"Are you allergic to any metals?" asked Drew, to which Marvelry shook his head. Drew examined the watch, flipping it over to discover a sticky residue, which seemed to be oozing from the back. "What the heck is this?"

Marvelry didn't respond, as he had already fallen fast asleep.

Drew looked back at the watch, wondering what was really taking place at the Sundown estate.

At dinner that evening Drew filled everyone in on Marvelry's condition.

"Poor Julian," said Barnaby, in dismay. "He's missing out on all the fun."

"What's the matter with him?" asked Nick.

"I don't know," said Drew. "He seems to be getting worse, though."

"He seemed perfectly fine when he got here," said Drood, who had been sitting silently at the end of the table.

"He's getting on in years," said Nick. "He'll never be as alive and full of vigor as when he was on stage performing. I worry myself that my spirit may wither without the drive to be at my very best every night."

Drood suddenly excused himself. A few minutes later, Drew left the table himself, wanting to know where the old man was headed. When Drew reached the second floor he saw Drood leaving Marvelry's room, and then proceeding on to his own room a few doors down. Drew rushed into Marvelry's room to check on him. The older man's eyes were closed, his face was exceedingly pale, and it seemed as if he wasn't breathing. Fortunately, when Drew got closer to the bed, he could see Marvelry's diaphragm rise and fall, and hear his hoarse respiration.

Drew went back to the door and opened it slightly. He peeked out into the hall and saw Drood heading back downstairs. As soon as he was out of sight, Drew crept out and hurried into Drood's unlocked room.

The room was similar to his own. A large, black cloak hung from the back of the door, and a mortar and pestle sat on the dresser. Drew noted that there was some remaining residue in the bowl. He stepped closer to investigate, when the door suddenly swung open and Drood rushed in.

"What are you doing in here?" asked Drood, threateningly.

"What were *you* doing in Dr. Marvelry's room?" replied Drew.

"I was checking on him."

"Why?" demanded Drew. He assumed the magician was trying to work his way out of a lie.

"He's got all the telltale signs of a poisoning. Dizziness. Nausea. Weak limbs. I just wish I knew *what* was poisoning him," said Drood.

"When I was walking around yesterday, Barnaby told me to stay away from some flowers in the garden. He said you told him they were poisonous. Do you think Dr. Marvelry could have come into contact with them?"

Drood's eyes grew wide and his fleshy jaw dropped. "Wolfsbane! It's true; it's a highly dangerous plant. And it can cause symptoms similar to what Dr. Marvelry is experiencing. But I'm certain he's never set foot in Nick's garden. Plus, if he touched wolfsbane, he'd have a nasty rash to prove it."

"I saw a red mark on his wrist, when he took off his watch. It looked like the kind you might get from poison ivy."

"Really?" asked Drood, intrigued.

"Yeah. And his watch had some kind of sticky residue on the back," said Drew. He paused, remembering a small detail from the previous day. "There's one more thing."

"Yes?"

"I saw some flower petals that may have been wolfsbane on an apothecary bench in Nick's basement."

"Did they look like this?" Drood asked, showing him the bowl which sat on his dresser.

Drew nodded.

"I found a few petals in the kitchen and I decided to test them." Drood pulled up his sleeve, revealing two red, rashy lines on his forearm. "When Nick invited Marvelry to his estate, I was confused. Anybody who worked with them back in their heyday knew that Nick *hated* Marvelry with a passion. When Marvelry retired, he was the best in the business; he went out on top. Nick was upset for years that he never had a chance to surpass him."

"So you think Nick is poisoning Dr. Marvelry?"

"Yes, I do. I had a hunch, but I didn't know how. He must have rigged the watch to release the flower extract gradually, so as to not stir up any suspicion."

Drew couldn't fathom that his idol could commit such a deed. "Is there a treatment for wolfsbane poisoning?"

"There's nothing that will immediately reverse the effects of the poison—prolonged exposure has been known to lead to heart and organ failure. His condition should improve if he stays out of contact with the toxin, and the affected area is thoroughly washed."

They hurried to Marvelry's room and woke him. With haste, they undressed him and put him in the shower. When Marvelry was out and dressed, they explained the situation—the poisoning mechanism, how Nick's retirement party had been a cover for a deadly form of payback.

"I can't believe it," said Marvelry, who was still quite sickly. "I've been out of the business for years. Why would he still hold a grudge?"

Drood paced around the room. "Bastard. I say we run down to that swank dining room of his and teach him a lesson."

Drew, enraged by Nickleby's treachery, nodded in agreement.

"Hold on, hold on!" said Marvelry, attempting to calm the pair. "Don't be rash...I've got a better idea for our friend. Since removing the watch this afternoon I believe my condition has improved. Let's sleep on this."

*　　　*　　　*

"Nick, come quick! Dr. Marvelry needs help!" yelled Drew as he entered the dining room, startling Barnaby and Nick, who were sitting down for a quiet breakfast.

"What's wrong?" asked Nick.

"We found him lying on the carpet, barely breathing," added Drew.

Nick stood quickly and hustled toward the door. "Dear, god!"

"I'll call an ambulance," said Drood, running out of the room.

Drew followed Nick, hurrying up to Marvelry's room, Barnaby in tears behind them. When they entered the room Marvelry was lying on the bed, eyes closed. The group gathered around him; Barnaby grabbed at Marvelry and wailed. Nick paced and tried to advise Drew on resuscitative methods, to no avail. Nobody had the slightest idea what to do.

The hanging dread of the room was interrupted by the arrival of an ambulance outside. Soon there was the pounding of footsteps in the hallway and a pair of medics rushed in, ordering everyone to leave the room.

Drew, Nick and Barnaby walked out to the hall and listened as the medics went to work. Drood joined them, putting his ear against the door in anticipation. Everyone gasped when they heard the female medic say, "Time of death: 9:24 a.m." The group rushed back into the room to find their friend lying on a stretcher, covered completely by a sheet. Barnaby practically fell to the floor in agony over the scene.

"Is he...gone?" asked Nick.

"Can't you do CPR?" Drew demanded.

"We tried, sir; I'm afraid this man was dead when we got here," said the other medic.

Drew collapsed to his knees, tears streaming from his eyes. Drood and Barnaby helped him to his feet and carried him out of the room, leaving Nick and the two medics alone with the body. The technicians were about to wheel the stretcher away when Nick said, "Wait, can I have a minute with my friend?"

Both medics left the room and Nick stood next to the stretcher, his mournful expression slowly twisting into a smile. "I've waited for this day for a long time; when I would no longer have to live in the shadow of Dr. Marvelry, the *greatest illusionist the world has ever seen*. You were nothing before I brought you out on the road, but I watched as you gradually stole my audience. I was making my great comeback, ready to eclipse you, but you quit, robbing me of the opportunity. Now, it's over. You're gone and I can finally, deservedly, be called the greatest illusionist in the—"

"Once a magician, always a liar," said a voice from behind Nick, startling him. He whipped his head around to see Marvelry standing there, arms crossed, grinning.

136

"How-how?" stammered Nick, eyes wide in disbelief at the pallid ghoul before him. He looked back at the stretcher and then at the older gentleman. Nick's face quickly turned red and he stomped his feet on the floor in rage. Marvelry stood resolute, as he had done on thousands of stages around the world.

Nick whipped back around and ripped the sheet off the stretcher. When he saw who was underneath, he shuddered. There lay Claudia, a triumphant smile on her face.

"*You're* in on this too?!" said Nick, his voice shaky, defeated.

"Nick, you should know by now that the eyes lie. I knew you wouldn't touch my 'corpse' out of superstition. Had you done so you would have discovered our deception. A well-practiced illusionist sees with his hands, after all," said Marvelry, as the rest of his assistants for the "act"—Drew, Drood, and the two medics—swooped in to restrain Nick, the *second*-greatest magician in the world.

APPENDIX

AN ARTICLE ON DR. MARVELRY
FROM THE SUN PRESS

Objects of Affection

Famed local magician Dr. Marvelry talks career, retirement and lost love

By GREG DOUGLAS, gdouglas@sunpress.com

BINGHAMPTON, NY -- A pair of silver shoes. That's what got the great Dr. Marvelry talking.

For those unfamiliar with the man (of which, I'm sure the number is few), Dr. Marvelry is arguably Binghampton's most famous son. A magician from the city's north side, Marvelry made the world his stage for decades, dazzling audiences from Canton to Calcutta with never-before-seen tricks and illusions. His legend looms large around the world and right here in his hometown (have you driven down Marvelry Way lately?)

Despite his worldwide acclaim, however, Marvelry as a man remains very much a mystery. What is his real name? Who is he, really? How did he go from store clerk to worldwide superstar, and what was the reason for his sudden retirement?

Marvelry hasn't given a proper interview since the curtain closed on his last performance over twenty years ago. It was a family connection which afforded me the opportunity to speak with the prestidigitator. Regina Beck, my deceased aunt, was Marvelry's long-time assistant. Over the years, my mother revealed small details about my aunt's relationship with the man, but the topic was usually relegated to hushed, adult conversations. The magician's much-discussed recent appearance at the Thomas A. Zopp Cystic Fibrosis Awareness Dinner (see Page 1A, 3/4/16), however, inspired me to finally seek him out.

The story of my first meeting with Marvelry begins with a pair of silver slippers, which I brought to him at his peculiar antique store, Marvelry's Curiosity Shop, located on Clinton Street's famous Antique Row. He is a genial man in his mid-sixties, and enjoys the small details and peculiar stories that accompany each item in his shop. Most millennials of the Binghampton area remember the Curiosity Shop from childhood as a place to purchase party favors, decorations, and magician's implements. Marvelry changed with the times and competition, and grew his shop into a popular antique store which services a growing, niche clientele seeking strange, often forgotten items from the past.

The silver slippers which I gave to Marvelry, at my mother's request, had been in the possession of my aunt at the time of her sudden death. Marvelry was happy to receive them, having believed that Regina had tossed them into the San Francisco Bay before their final performance at the famed Orpheum Theater. He became animated at the sight of the shoes and told me of his and Regina's first meeting.

"I had seen her window shopping across the street at what used to be a fashionable clothing store," said Marvelry. "I couldn't quite figure out the item she was fixated on, but she caught my attention from the first moment I saw her. I knew a teen girl wasn't going to come into a hardware store, so I would volunteer for deliveries, hoping for a chance to run into her. And one day, unbeknownst to me, she followed me on a delivery and then back into the store. We struck up a lasting friendship from that point on."

It was the 1970s and Marvelry was working at the hardware store owned by his father, Ralph Marvilynov. The store was shuttered upon his father's death, and it was decades later that the Curiosity Shop came into existence, in the very same spot. Marvelry had been a world traveler and college graduate before he had entered into the performance trade, and said that Regina inspired him to make the leap to the stage.

"When I finally returned to Binghampton, I was back working in the hardware store for the summer, and was about to start my new job as a math teacher at Binghampton High," stated Marvelry. "Regina came around and we dated a little, and she really liked the new tricks I had picked up in the Orient. I had gotten her the silver shoes years before, and she would wear them out with me. She was the one who really encouraged me to try magic as a profession. When my dad had his stroke and passed, we closed the hardware store and I couldn't stand to be around. I worked as a carnival barker and traveled the country for some time before meeting the Illustrious Dante, who would become my mentor. I was his assistant and he taught me the basics of the illusionist's craft, and we became quite successful on the small, regional circuits."

It was only a few years before Marvelry had mastered the art form and been recognized by one of the biggest magicians in the world, Nick Nickleby. "My mentor, Dante, retired to Europe and I got a few lucky breaks, and created the right tricks at the right time, and found myself in New York City opening for Nick. Regina came to the show, which was really a great surprise. I didn't know she had moved to the city, and she was wearing the silver shoes. It was my most memorable performance," said Marvelry. "All I cared about was impressing her. We were together for years after that, traveling from city to city with the Great American Virtuosos, where I was a featured performer and Regina worked as a costume seamstress."

Eventually, Marvelry outgrew his contemporaries and was headlining shows the world over, performing for queens, princes, and heads of state, from London to Tokyo. My aunt became his full-time assistant, performing alongside him and becoming a bit of a star herself. "She was a great student. I was obsessed with honing my craft, studying mechanical illusions, and I was completely enamored with her," said Marvelry.

Tragically, for my aunt, there was a price that came along with the fame. During their final three-show, sold-out run at the Orpheum in 1989, growing differences in lifestyle caused tension between the pair. Regina had immersed herself in the seedier side of the entertainment business, partying heavily, picking up a drug habit, which alarmed Marvelry, who favored a more tranquil life beyond the stage.

"I knew she was drifting, but I thought I could handle keeping her and the show together. I was wrong," said Marvelry. "After the first night, we met up with some of the city's finest poets, composers, and writers. That is what I miss most of the traveling show, sharing ideas with geniuses, shapers of our cultural landscape. Regina wasn't as moved by Ginsberg and Warhol as I was. She preferred to keep company with the musicians and their scene."

Marvelry was very open with me about his and my aunt's last few days together, for which I am forever grateful.

"We had to have a discussion about our future. She left after the argument and I didn't see her until the following afternoon," said Marvelry. "While we were setting up the stage for the last performance, she walked in barefoot in costume, and I asked her where her silver shoes were. It was her trademark. Regina had fans that were uniquely her own. Young girls were drawn to her and her look. She said she had thrown them in the bay. So she performed barefoot and it was a train wreck of a show; she missed most of her marks. I did all I could do to get through it and to keep the audience from walking out. After the show we argued again; she seemed completely lost. She went out again with her new entourage, and I searched for her for hours, before finding her on some hotel balcony—but it was too late."

From that point on, Marvelry was done performing. He returned to Binghampton and pursued a doctorate in mythology, authenticating his stage name. He opened the Curiosity Shop at his father's old storefront.

Appendix

It's not often in a journalist's career that he gets to report on something so personal. When I returned my aunt's silver shoes to Marvelry, he seemed thrilled at the mere fact of their existence. It was with glee that he revealed to me what she had written inside one of the shoes: "Julian '72"—next to a hand-drawn heart.

A DARK AND DESOLATE RECURRENCE

(Preview from our upcoming fall 2016 anthology – *At The Cemetery Gates: Year One*)

"**A**t this rate, we'll never get out of here," said Teddy Mealer, gritting his teeth as he yanked the steering wheel of his compact car and laid on the gas. His Prius, as it turned out, wasn't built for blizzard-level conditions in the Catskills, and he was reminded of that fact every time his engine roared in a vain attempt to retreat from the large snowbank.

"Don't say that, honey," replied his wife, Margo. She looked out in fear at the snow piled up against her window. It was a vision of white on all sides of the car. Each window was suffocated by snow, save for a hint of an opening out the rear window.

"I don't think you understand, babe. I can't move. I think we're stuck here."

A panicked look crossed Margo's face. "Are you serious?" She nudged the handle on her door, then proceeded to yank it and kick at the door before her husband restrained her.

Teddy shook his head. "You're wasting your time. I'll keep trying, but I don't think it'll do any good. We're packed like sardines."

Nearly a half-hour passed and Teddy was unable to free the car from the clutches of the cold, white mass. He punched the steering wheel in frustration. "We're nearly out of gas. We've got to get out of here soon or we'll freeze. Or worse, there's the whole carbon monoxide thing."

Margo took her cell phone out of her purse for the third time in ten minutes, but she couldn't get a signal. "Teddy, I'm scared. What are we going to do?"

"I don't know." There was a newfound weariness to his voice, as if the dread that his wife was experiencing had finally caught up with him.

Margo was about to throw a fit when she heard the roar of another engine. She looked outside to see the headlights of a large, black pickup with an attached plow pull up behind their car. The front door opened and out stepped a bearded, middle-aged man in a brown parka and dungarees.

"Ted, I think this guy's going to help us out!" Margo beamed. She took her husband's hand and squeezed it in excitement.

"Thank god."

They watched as the man took a chain and attached it somewhere underneath their car. He returned to his truck and gunned it in reverse. Teddy and Margo let out a mutual sigh of relief as their car creaked back and forth stubbornly, then slipped out of the snowbank and onto the road.

The man got out of his truck again, detached the chain from their car, and threw it back onto the bed. He stopped and looked inside at the couple for a brief second before getting into his vehicle. Teddy and Margo watched as their good Samaritan drove away.

"What a nice man," said Margo. "He didn't even ask for anything. Didn't even wait around for a thank-you."

"People out here look out for one another," said Teddy. "That's a good guy, there."

Teddy went to drive away, but the car wouldn't move. They were out of the bank, but the vehicle was immobile. "Son of a bitch! What now?"

Margot was agonizingly silent.

"It feels like the rear axle might be broke. Shit—why'd that guy have to leave in such a hurry? I mean, he was a big help and all, but where'd he go?" said Ted. He forced his door open and looked down the road, but all he could see was a dense, white snow fog. He examined the rear of the car and, sure enough, the wheel was crooked because the axle was broken.

Teddy returned to the car and sighed. With their gas tank almost empty, the couple decided that they would have to leave the Prius behind and seek shelter. They stepped out of the vehicle and were instantly struck by the frigid, winter air. They walked for only a minute before they noticed a small cabin set back a few hundred yards from the road. They decided to head for it and to ask whoever lived there if they could come inside. It was beginning to grow dark, so they trudged onward into the foot-high snow.

Teddy and Margo arrived at a modest cabin. There was a small porch attached to the front, on which sat Adirondack chairs, snow piled up on each seat. A wide, stone chimney jutted out just off to one side of the porch, many of the stones having fallen to the ground nearby. They stepped onto the porch and wood cracked beneath their feet.

Teddy knocked repeatedly on the door, but no one answered. He turned the doorknob and felt that it wasn't locked.

He called out before they ventured inside. "Hello? Is anybody home?"

No one answered. The icy wind howled through the evergreens behind them.

"I guess not," said Margo.

With the cold snapping against their faces, the couple felt they had no other option but to enter. As they passed through the doorway, they were immediately taken aback by a sharp musty smell.

"*Ugh*, Teddy. That *smell*. Who the heck lives here? Don't they clean?"

"I don't think anyone's lived here for years. Or it might be a poorly kept hunting cabin – this is deer country, after all," said Teddy. He looked around. They were standing in a small living room which had a loft area above. There was a TV and a sofa, which was adorned with a blanket, on which was stitched a grey wolf howling at the moon. A large mirror hung over the sofa.

The living room led into a kitchen with a modest-sized refrigerator and stove, and a table for two. The kitchen had the sole working light on the first floor, which hung from a string, and shone into the living room. Cobwebs covered every corner and piece of furniture in the cabin; crunchy leaves and various forest debris were scattered about the floor.

"It's like they just ran out and left everything behind," said Margo.

Teddy found a book of matches inside a kitchen drawer and used it to light a fire in a small wood stove in the corner of the living room. Kindling and enough wood for the night was set conveniently near the entranceway. He took a seat next to Margo on the sofa and they held each other to keep warm until the room reached a bearable temperature.

Worn out from their ordeal on the road and the trek to the cabin, they quickly fell asleep on the stranger's sofa.

They hadn't slept twenty minutes when Margo tapped Teddy on the shoulder. "What's that noise?" she asked.

There was a heavy pounding on the loft floor above, as if someone were stomping around. They listened with intense curiosity as one set of footsteps traveled down from the loft, followed by a second, heavier set.

Margo tucked her head into her husband's shoulder. "Oh, my god, somebody's inside. Maybe the owners came home."

"Don't you think they would have come in through the front door? Maybe saw us on the couch and woke us up? Why would they be running up and down the steps?" said Teddy. "It might be some rats, or raccoons, or something. Who knows what openings or broken windows there might be in an old, forgotten place like this."

Teddy was about to lay his head back against the cushion when he heard what was unmistakably a human scream. It was that of a woman, and she kept repeating the same word in a frenzied tone, over and over. "*No, no, no!*"

Neither of them moved. The screaming continued, traveling from upstairs to downstairs, growing louder, more intense with each passing minute. This continued for another ten minutes, when suddenly, as if someone had flicked a switch, it stopped. No more screaming, no more footsteps. The sound gone, all they could hear was the creaking of the house and the whistling of the wind outside.

"What was that?!" whispered Margo, her face tense.

"I don't know. It sounded like someone being chased around. But I didn't see a thing."

"Teddy, is this place *haunted?*" Margo couldn't believe she was asking such a question, or that she half-considered it a possibility.

They discussed leaving the cabin for a moment but realized they still couldn't venture outside. Not until morning at least. The snowfall had waned, but the wind had picked up considerably.

Hungry, they searched the kitchen for food. Margo opened the refrigerator and nearly vomited at the pungent, death-like smell that wafted out. Undefined molds lined the drawers and compartments. She quickly slammed the door.

Teddy had a little more luck. He managed to scrounge up a couple cans of fruit cocktail from a lower cabinet that were less than a year past expiration. He found a can opener and they shared the meager portion.

Their bellies as full as they would get for the night, and the cabin now comfortably warm, Teddy and Margo climbed the stairs to the loft to explore. The closet fixture held the only working bulb in the loft, and it shone a comfortable glow into the bedroom. The bed was unmade, and it looked as if the sheets had been thrown on the floor in a fit. A pair of panties and a pair of boxers were strewn with some other faded articles of clothing.

"It looks like a couple lives here. Or should I say 'lived' here," said Teddy.

They flipped the mattress and dug a clean, moth-bitten bedsheet out from a dresser, then laid down together. They were sound asleep minutes later.

"No! No! Oh, god, no! It doesn't mean anything! I love you! Oh, please don't hurt him!"

Margo let out an awful cry as she awoke, the shrill woman's voice again echoing through the cabin. She looked at her husband's watch. She and Teddy hadn't been sleeping twenty minutes.

"What the fuck *is* that?" asked Teddy. "I'm going to check it out."

"No," said Margo, throwing herself over her husband. "Please don't leave me."

This time, they heard the pounding coming from the staircase and traveling toward the bed. The couple screamed as the bed lifted off the ground a few inches and crashed back down to the floor. The footsteps traveled from the loft, down to the kitchen, and possibly all the way to the basement. This time, the chaos ended with a loud "*ka-pow*," as if someone had fired a gun. Then another "*ka-pow*." Then silence.

Tears streamed down Margo's face. "Let's go. Oh, god, let's get out of here!" She ran out of the bed and down the stairs, ready to bolt out the front door, but Teddy chased after her and blocked the doorway.

"Where are you going?" he asked.

"Ted, this place is haunted. I'm scared!"

He held her tight by the shoulders and nodded. "Okay, okay. I believe you. I think it's haunted, too. Some repetitive haunting is taking place here. Every hour or so. I heard about this kind of thing watching all those seasons of *Ghost Stalkers*. Someone who dies under extreme circumstances often ends up repeating the events leading up to their death, over and over again. I think someone was murdered here, and it's playing out like the cabin has the awful memory imprinted on it."

"Then let's go! Why are you standing there if you know what's coming!"

"Because it's a goddamn blizzard out there, and we'll die if we spend an hour in it. It's two in the morning and we're miles from anywhere. Nobody's going to stop by. That nice guy with the truck is long gone."

"So what do we do, Teddy?"

"I don't think the ghosts can harm us. They're dead and simply re-enacting a scene; we're just observers. Those poor bastards.

Could you imagine being forced to re-live the same horrible event forever?"

Realizing the bed in the loft played a major part in the haunting, Teddy convinced Margo to return to the couch on the first floor. They weren't going to get much sleep anyway.

Sure enough, an hour later the haunting commenced again. The bed in the loft, the pounding footsteps descending downstairs to the kitchen, through the living room. Then the two gunshots. But Teddy and Margo weren't safer in the living room, as it turned out. As the night wore on, more chaos unfolded. They watched in horror as objects flew across the room—clothes, pillows, books. They were forced to duck and dive as some of the room's heavier objects arced through the air—a lamp, dishes, at one point a small television.

Teddy held Margo close beneath the wolf blanket. They were too frightened to keep tending to the fire. They shivered through the hours as the horrors seemingly escalated. It was a form of torture, one they dreaded more as each minute passed, knowing that the next repetition would be more intense, more violent.

Teddy was nodding off during one of the lulls between repetitions, the sun just beginning to make its presence known through the dirty windows, when Margo let out a wild scream. He watched as his wife was lifted into the air. She clutched at her throat, trying to tear away an invisible pair of hands. Her face was straining and turning a shade of purple. He jumped up and threw his body into the phantom perpetrator. Teddy connected with the unseen force and Margo fell to the floor, gasping for air.

Teddy looked up and saw the reflection of a man running away in the mirror over the couch. Although it was still pretty dark, with a little light from the bulb in the kitchen, he could have sworn it was the same man in the brown parka and dungarees who towed their car out of the snowbank.

Footsteps pounded down to the basement again. Then the two gunshots that ended it all. But this time a third shot rang out, just moments later.

That was all the Mealers could take. They ran outside. The orange rays of the sun had just begun peeking over the mountains. The storm had died down and the air was noticeably warmer.

"I think I figured out what happened," said Teddy, out of breath from the exertion. "The man who lived there killed his wife. The underwear on the floor? I think he caught her in bed with another man and chased them around the house. It all ended in the basement, where he shot them both and then himself—the third shot."

Margo nodded in silence as they swiftly left the cabin behind, post holing through the deep snow. She didn't care who killed who; she just wanted to go home.

"I think the guy with the pickup was the one who killed them," stated Teddy. "Honey, I think we got pulled out of a ditch by a *ghost*."

They made it back to the road, hoping they could flag down a passing motorist and hitch a ride into town. As they neared the scene of their accident, they were surprised to see the car was no longer sitting where they had abandoned it – it was firmly lodged in the snowbank. They stopped dead in their tracks when it was clear that the same black pickup from the night before was pulling their Prius free.

"Honey, that ghost. He's back again," said Teddy.

They stood silently, watching as the man in the brown parka and dungarees exited his truck to retrieve the chains. The man then looked into the driver-side window of their car, shook his head and jogged back toward his truck – shouting back over his shoulder, "I live just up ahead. I'll go call an ambulance!"

Margo and Teddy walked over to the Prius as the truck tore down the road. They couldn't believe their eyes. There they were, sitting in the front seat, their faces ghastly white. They were dead, long dead.

"Teddy. What?! Who are those people?" Margo's lip quivered. A nasty wind whipped against her face. "They look like…"

"Us. That's because it *is* us, honey. We're dead. That guy was the killer. See him driving away? He's going to go find his wife in bed with another man and kill them both. Don't you see? He returned home early because he was going to go call us an ambulance. He didn't know we were dead. We're just like him, repeating our episode."

ACKNOWLEDGMENTS

Thanks to Burt and Pete for providing us with invaluable feedback on the book. Sybil for putting up with us while we spent countless hours in the living room reading these stories out loud. Ben Baldwin for designing an amazing cover and bringing Marvelry to life. Zinger for keeping our spirits high. And our devilishly wonderful children.

35053319R00094

Made in the USA
Middletown, DE
17 September 2016